ALSO BY
CLAY McLEOD CHAPMAN

KILL YOUR DARLING

CLAY McLEOD CHAPMAN

Bad Hand Books
www.badhandbooks.com

For William A. Henshaw,
"a writer of little consequence,"
and Ann Robinson Henshaw,
who taught me how to read.

In writing, you must kill all your darlings.
—William Faulkner

DUCT TAPE TO FAMILY TIME

They wrapped a whole roll of duct tape around his head. Really layered him up good and thick, all the way down to the cardboard spool.

Whoever suffocated my son sealed him inside his own pressure-sensitive shell. No light, no sound. Sure as hell wasn't any air. Billy would've been breathing in polyethylene for those last few minutes of his life, the thrum of his own jackrabbit heartbeat pounding against his eardrums.

His eyelids were glued against the adhesive side of the tape. Couldn't blink without pulling his eyelashes out. Soaked in his own sweat. Trapped in that skull-sized sauna.

The surface of the tape bubbled with each muffled scream. Nothing but these pockets of trapped carbon dioxide blistering around his head, pulsing in odd spots. Every exhale was looking for an escape, not finding one.

Here's the real kicker: Across the surface, directly over top of Billy's own eyes, were two black circles. Whoever did this to him pulled out a permanent marker and laced the taped-over craters of Billy's sockets with a pair of uneven eyes.

Cartoon things, really. The left circle was larger than the right. No irises, no retinas. Just two sloppy, lopsided ovals staring blankly out at nothing.

A child's drawing. On my fifteen-year-old son.

How do you stop yourself from seeing these things?

I want to know.

I'm asking here. *Really*. I can't stop myself from dwelling on *maximum adhesion* all the time.

All-weather durability.

Super flexibility.

High-tensile strength for a long-lasting hold.

Whenever I'm at the hardware store, I'm comparing brands just to see if I can't figure out which kind they used on my boy.

Would these bastards pick up the standard brand? Or would they save a few cents and use a knock-off?

I want to believe they'd only use the best for Billy.

I keep hearing that high-pitched squeal of tape peeling off the roll. Only it doesn't stop. It's on a permanent loop now, yard after yard winding around his head.

We're talking every day for forty years now.

Forty years. Let that thought settle in for a second…

Forty goddamn years.

It's a surprisingly sly sound. Fabric ripping. Curtains tearing at my back. Shirts splitting at the seams. Follows me around wherever I go. I can hear it just about anywhere. Over my shoulder at the grocery store. In the neighboring aisle.

At night, I'll close my eyes, only a few breaths away from finally drifting off—

And there it is, waiting for me. That shrill *zzzip* tearing away from the rest of the roll. When my eyes bolt open, I expect to see the adhesive side of a silver strip coming my way, blacking out my vision.

But there's nothing there. Nobody's leaning over my bed.

Nothing.

How can I stop myself from seeing these things in my sleep? That silver-gray moon orbiting my son's cranium, making its rotations like his head is its own planet.

Round and round and round…

You've got to figure a guy can get a solid twenty or thirty revolutions around somebody's head from just one roll before it's all unspooled.

Guess again.

Thirty-eight.

It took thirty-eight laps around my son's skull.

Thirty-eight spins around the sun before hitting cardboard. Ain't nothing getting through that.

Rather than unwrap the duct tape from his head, the medical examiner had to take his surgical scissors and cut through the bloody clump in two separate spots.

(*snip-snip*)

Once behind each ear. He tugged the two collapsible halves apart like my son was a pistachio nut.

Your first simile, I can hear my workshop instructor congratulating me. When I asked him what the hell a simile was, he explained to me that *it makes the object you're writing about more vivid for the reader. They can see it better in their mind.*

That last layer of tape kept its grip on his skin. The coroner had to peel it off just to reach his face.

His swollen cheeks.

His purple eyelids. Like bruised fruit.

A pummeled orange.

Is this what you want to see? Feels pretty vivid to me. There's plenty more where that came from. I'm swimming in similes. I can't stop myself from seeing them now, all around me. Hearing them wherever I go. They're everywhere.

Every story worth its salt begins with a solid hook.

So saideth our workshop instructor from the get-go.

You must grab your reader's attention from the very

first sentence, he told our class on day number one. *Don't ever let them go.*

There was a thin bedding of blonde hair clinging to the adhesive side. Plucked a couple of eyelashes out—I already told you that. I saw for myself when I got called in to identify his body. My boy's body. My son. The tape hadn't been placed into evidence yet, just lying there on a metal tray by the examination table.

The asphyxiating shell had retained the shape of his head. A silver-gray mask of my son.

These are the thoughts I had, looking at him. Continue to have. These are the kinds of thoughts that don't ever go away.

They never go away. These thoughts are even older than my son now. I've had them longer than I had him.

Forty years. Haunted by duct tape. Silver-gray ghosts.

In the morgue, I ran my finger down the tacky side of the tape. That was a big no-no. What's that called? I'm a writer now, right? I should know the proper names for these things. Devil's in the details. I need to do my research. What was it?

Tampering with evidence? Corrupting a DNA sample?

I needed to feel the downiness of his uprooted hair, the hair that had gotten caught in the duct tape, tugged up from his scalp when they pried the mask off him.

That softness. His hair across my fingertips.

And there it was, just like it was yesterday, a wave smashing into me…

Billy's first haircut.

I'd taken him to the barbershop just before his second birthday. The barber helped him up into the chair, giving him a booster seat and wrapping an apron around his neck. Stuffed this tissue paper around his throat and got clipping.

(snip-snip)

Billy wouldn't stop wailing. His face purpled up from all the crying. Every time those scissors came near his ears, his shoulders would pop up to block them.

It's a miracle the barber made it through without any defensive wounds.

Billy's head was so small. Barely even a grapefruit back then.

Just a boy. Always a boy.

Never a man.

I remember eyeing the linoleum around the barber chair. Watched the bits of his blonde hair fall to the floor. They drifted down so slowly. A golden snow flurry.

I went ahead and leaned over. Pinched a loose lock from the floor. A keepsake for our family scrapbook.

The Book of Billy. His life, mounted on construction paper, complete with a burgundy red faux leatherette cover and gold stamping.

Every pivotal moment of his life was sealed safely behind cellophane.

Billy's birth certificate.

Billy's footprint.

Billy's first day back home from the hospital.

Billy's first pony ride.

Billy's first Halloween.

Billy's first birthday.

Billy's first tooth.

Billy's first Christmas.

I taped the lock of his hair to the page and wrote right below it:

Billy's first haircut, 1975.

Flip to the first page and you can see it for yourself. A little sprig of wheat, dried out after all these years. The tape still has its grip, though. It won't let him go.

How's that for a hook?

ADULT CREATIVE WRITING WORKSHOP!

The Patterson main library will be hosting a weekly creative writing workshop. Engage your imagination, your senses, and your words!

Work with a professional, published author to tell the story you were born to tell. Refreshments offered!

Six sessions. Thursday nights, October 5th to November 2nd. 6 to 8 PM.

Adults only. Registration required. Interested parties can sign up at the front desk.

Tell the story you're dying to tell!

FIND YOUR VOICE

The writing workshop was my wife's idea. To help *express myself*, she said. Unlock all the dogged thoughts I got rattling around up here.

Everybody's got at least one good book in them, so my book's about Billy.

I am the bard of my boy.

Let's be honest… Carol just wants me out of the house. That's all this is about. She's had her fill of me moping around our home. She steps into the living room, thinking she's the only one there. It isn't until I clear my throat that she even realizes I'm sitting in my armchair. Scares the living daylights out of her.

"You don't say hello now?" She asks. "Nearly gave me a heart attack…"

"Sorry."

"Why didn't you say something?"

"Thought you knew."

"I need to put a bell around your neck."

"I'll announce myself next time," I say. "*Your husband's over here!*"

"What're you doing in the dark?" She shuffles over to the light switch, bringing some light into the room. "Solving the world's problems?"

"Just thinking, is all."

Just thinking has been my go-to for years now. We both know what that means.

Just thinking about Billy.

Just thinking about that night.

Just thinking about what they did to him.

Just thinking about who it was. Who it could've been. Who could do something like that.

Who.

Carol knows to leave me alone when I'm *just thinking*. We have our own secret codes. Our signals for one another.

Don't think I'm the only one, now. She's got hers, too.

I'm gonna take a nap…

I need to close my eyes for a spell…

I'm gonna rest my head…

Carol sleeps while I just think.

She would have slept through the last four decades if she could've. She'd prefer to be in a coma. Just close her eyes, all those years ago, and never wake up.

Carol blames me for what happened.

That's all right by me.

I blame her, too.

We go back and forth. Sometimes, I'll take the blame for a stretch. Then she'll shoulder it. It's an odd volley between us. Back and forth, like that.

You let him go.

Back and forth...

You told him he could stay out late.

Back and forth...

You didn't get worried enough, even when he didn't come home.

Back and forth...

You didn't go looking for him.

Back and forth...

You didn't call the cops. Why didn't you call the cops?

Back and forth...

You. You. You.

Back. Forth.

Back again.

There's enough to go around between us. Every nit-picking minute from that night needs to be accounted for. Every little detail atoned for.

We've only got each other to blame.

Nobody else.

When the cops didn't arrest anyone, we went ahead and arrested each other. I've been on trial for decades now.

And now, I've been sentenced to *express myself.*

I'm staring at this flyer on the coffee table. She'd

left it there without saying a word, knowing I'd stumble across it sooner or later.

This is how we communicate with one another now. Particularly on matters where we don't actually want to talk to each other. There are Post-It notes clinging to cabinet doors and lampshades, feathering the whole house in yellow reminders.

Pick up milk. Phone bill is overdue. Pilot went out.

But this flyer sure was a curve ball.

Just glancing at the goddamn thing gave me a migraine. Photocopied on fluorescent orange paper. There was a hole at the top. From a push pin, I could tell. Carol must've spotted the flyer somewhere. Ten bucks says it came from the community corkboard at the front of the grocery store, right where the sliding glass door opens up. She must've pulled it down before all the slots filled up.

This punishment cost Carol $250.00. Over forty bucks an hour. And for what? Somebody teaching me how to *express myself*?

This has got to be a joke, I thought. No—that's not true. My first thought was:

What's Carol done to me?

"I'm turning seventy-seven. The hell am I gonna do in a creative writing class?"

"Think of it as an early birthday present," she says. "Get outta your head for once."

"Out of my head? Where else should I be? Where else am I gonna go?"

"Get your head out of your ass," she suggests. "How's that? Better?"

"I'm not doing it."

"Too late. Already signed you up."

"I'm not doing it!"

"What's it gonna hurt?"

Christ, everything hurt these days. Sneeze anywhere near me and it'll leave a bruise.

"You're doing it," she says. "Don't think you can get out of going."

I blame her broken hip.

Carol's the one who's been sentenced to bedrest—and here she is, kicking *me* out of the house. She had gotten up in the middle of the night a month or so ago, mistaking our staircase for the bathroom. When her foot couldn't find the floor, the rest of her went tumbling down twelve wooden steps, end over end, until her left leg smacked the cold concrete below.

Fractured her hip in two different places. The femoral neck snapped like a twig.

Carol called out to me for a full two hours. Spent the rest of the night on the floor, watching dawn seep through the living room window. Wet herself, too, this nimbus of piss radiating out from her nightgown. Two sunrises. But we don't talk about that.

When I woke, I noticed her side of the bed was empty. I figured Carol had gotten up already. Wouldn't be the first time I found myself alone.

"Glenn...?" She must have heard me shuffling

down the hall. "Glenn…" Her hoarse voice peeps up from down the steps. Raspy, but still her. Still Carol. "Glenn…"

"Where are you?"

"I'm down here."

"Where?"

"*Here.*"

I found her sprawled out on the ground floor like a tossed-off rag doll. Hair in her face. Nightgown undone, all soaked.

I couldn't pick her up. She was too heavy for me. I tried, but the strain went right to my back. "I'm sorry," I'd said. "I'm sorry. I can't do it… I have to call for help."

She nodded, silently assenting that my body had failed her.

Neither of us mentioned our honeymoon. How I had effortlessly carried her across the threshold then, way back when.

Whose bodies were these? These weakened things? One tumble and they break apart.

After calling for an ambulance, there was nothing left for us to do but wait. I lay next to Carol on the floor until the paramedics arrived, holding her hand in hopes of distracting her from the pain. I combed her hair from her face with my fingers. Smiled at her, finding her beautiful even then. She had suffered enough. Seven hours of shattered bones. I felt her shiver. The dampness had seeped right through. Her lips were a faint blue. And all I could do was smile like a fool.

"Don't worry," I'd said. "The ambulance is on its way. They'll be here soon."

"Soon," she answered back. Then, to herself, "Soon."

We spent the rest of the morning on the floor like two kids. We talked about Billy. Just waiting for the ambulance to arrive.

"Remember when he chased after the neighbor's dog?" I asked. "What was its name? Harold?"

"You're getting the names all wrong," Carol croaked, her voice so dry. "Harold was our neighbor. Their dog's name was Muffles."

"You sure about that?"

"Well, our neighbor's name sure wasn't Mr. Muffles…"

There are so few moments of clarity anymore. Those pristine moments in your life, where, no matter how much time has slipped by since, you'll always remember them. Like they happened just yesterday.

The day Billy was born. That's one. The moment I first laid eyes on him. Nothing but a baby bird, freshly hatched. He was resting in Carol's arms, still damp with afterbirth, giving those lungs of his their first workout. Just wailing away.

His wrists were so thin. Bird wings.

Looking at the two of them right then and there, Carol and William Henry Partridge, I made a vow to myself and God above and anyone else willing to listen…

I will protect this boy for as long as I live.

I will see him through this life.

I will navigate him through this world and all the challenges that come his way.

I will give him a roof over his head. Food to eat.

I will pick him up when he is tired.

I will carry him when he's weak.

I will do anything he asks of me. God help me, anything.

I will surrender my life to him if I have to.

Anything. Everything.

Took fifteen years to let him down.

Carol doesn't have to blame me. I'm doing a pretty good job at it, myself. The sentences we serve, the punishments we perform, are our own form of hell.

Why wait when we can suffer for our sins right here and now?

We have this empty house. His room is Carol's personal purgatory. She'll spend the rest of eternity in there without him. Knowing that he's gone. Unable to touch anything. Just staring at the posters on the wall. The models of battleships we built. The die-cast cars. The perfectly made bed that hasn't been slept in for decades. Everything positioned in place. Carol has kept all his stuff looking just the way it did when Billy last touched it. As the custodian of our son's room, you'd better believe she'd know if something was moved out of place. Even by an inch.

The Museum of Our Son.

Every period of his life. Each epoch. All the artifacts of his existence are on display as if they were clay pots or primitive tools. Arrowheads. Corn husk dolls.

That's Carol's hell. Damned to curate this museum. Keep it clean. Dust it for eternity.

Me—my head is hell enough. The things I can't stop myself from seeing. The movies I play in my mind, projecting images across the back of my skull like it's a continuous movie reel—only instead of celluloid, this film strip is made of duct tape.

Hollywood's got nothing on me.

Carol and I don't share. They're just for us. Our own private purgatories.

But we've stayed together. Through it all. Through everything.

Our grief keeps us together.

We know when it's time to reach out to each other. We'll let the other suffer because it's our right to suffer—but if it's ever too much, the lifeline is cast out.

Whenever Carol slips too far into herself, too deep, I'll know. Her stare sinks into the back of her eyes. Lost somewhere. I'll know how to find her. Bring her back.

To our house. This life.

What life is left for us.

All I have to say is—*I miss him, too*—and she blinks back to me. In that moment, when her focus first returns and she finds me before her, welcoming her back with a smile, I'll catch a glimpse of her disappointment. It lingers in the back of her hazel eyes. This vague ray of sadness.

That's the exact moment when she realizes it's me. Not him.

We give each other our grief. There's love in heartache.

Try it sometime.

You wouldn't believe the bond it's built between us. Sure, sure, I've read plenty of statistics about how families can't survive the loss of a child.

What can I tell you? We did.

Enough of us did.

That's why this creative writing class cuts so deep. For the first time in years, Carol's telling me to get rid of my misery. As if she's sick of my sorrow.

Let go, she seems to be saying. *Let him go. Get him out of your system.*

"At least one of us should get out," she says. "Believe me, if I could take the class, I would… Better than being stranded in here with you all day."

The doctor sequestered Carol to our guest room on the ground floor. Until she heals, no more stairs. He's insisting on a hip replacement, but Carol won't listen.

I'm on convalescence duty and it's driving her up the wall. She can't stand me waiting on her hand and foot. She's had too much time to herself. To dwell.

I'm an easy target in this house.

"What will you do while I'm gone?" I ask.

"Who knows?" She shrugs. "Crosswords. Macramé. Possibilities are endless."

"But what if…" I waffle.

"What if *what*?"

"What if something happens to you? While I'm gone? What if I come home and find you on the floor again? Who'll be here to help you?"

"Jesus, Glenn… It's only one hour a week. It's just a class. You'll live."

You'll live.

I had lived. If Carol had her way, I knew she would swap me for him.

I would've.

"I'm not doing it," I say. "End of story."

"Just try it…"

"You can't make me. I won't."

"If you won't do it for yourself, then why not do it for me? How's that?"

I couldn't. Not for her.

Not for me.

For Billy, I nearly say. The words are right there, at the tip of my tongue. *I'll do it for Billy.*

ANYTHING NEW UNDER THE SUN

*E*very story has already been told.

Encouraging words from our workshop instructor.

"There is nothing new under the sun," he told us on day one. "There are no more original ideas, no new stories... There are only new ways of telling them."

I'm paying to listen to this bullshit?

Way to build morale, mister, I wanted to say, but I kept my trap shut.

Only six classes.

Six hours.

That landed me with... oh, five hours, fifty minutes to go.

But who's counting?

"The real question we must ask ourselves is..." He paused. Dramatic effect and all that. "*How am I going to tell my story?*"

I told my story to the police. I have held the Dade County Sheriff's Department hostage with my phone calls for decades.

"Give those poor men a rest," Carol insists. This was about a week before the flyer first made its appearance on our coffee table.

"Who?"

"You're still calling them," she says. "Don't act like you're not."

"I don't know what you're talking about…"

"You're a terrible liar."

"Call who? I'm not calling anybody…"

"Jesus, I can see right through you over the simplest fib."

"Who the hell am I gonna call?"

Sometimes I'd call two or three times a week, if I had a piece of information worth sharing. "I'm down to once a month," I lie. "Most months I don't even ring."

"Glenn. Your voice carries through the vents."

I wait until after Carol drifts off to sleep. When I figure she's not listening. That means most calls came in late at night, around ten thirty. Whatever skeleton crew is working the graveyard shift has to deal with me.

A typical exchange goes a little something like this…

"Dade County Sheriff's Department," the cop on call announces. No warmth to the welcoming. The voice is always efficient, to the bone.

I don't introduce myself anymore.

They know who it is.

Who I am.

"I'm calling to see if there's anything new on the Partridge case?"

"Mr. Partridge!" There's the warmth. Like a dam breaking through the receiver. That *ol' pal* familiarity pours right on through. Putting up with me. Tolerating me. You can practically hear the pity. Makes me sick to my stomach.

"How have you and Mrs. Partridge been? Everybody okay?"

"Fine. Fine." Now—down to business. "I think I might have found some important information that could be helpful for the case."

Case. As if there still was one.

"Sure thing," the voice on the other end will say. I can picture the smirk. In my head, it sounds like fingers rubbing over a balloon. That patronizing lift in their lips stretches out their words for an extra fraction of a second. Now they've got a salt- water-taffy tongue. "Hold on one sec. Let me get a pen. Make sure I get this down."

We follow the script, down to the pauses and platitudes, just like we've rehearsed this scene for all these years now. Never missing a beat.

It's just a game to them.

"I'll make sure Detective Corrigan gets this first thing in the morning."

"Thank you," I'll say.

"Want me to have her call when she comes in?"

"Yes. I'd appreciate it."

"You got it, Mr. Partridge. You have yourself a good night."

"Wait, before you go, could you tell the detective—"

—*that I think I may have found a bit of blood on his jacket. The shirt he was wearing that night is still in evidence. A few of his personal belongings were returned to us eventually, after they had been documented and catalogued, including his blue denim jacket. They wouldn't release his shirt to us because it was soiled. So much blood. But his jacket had been taken off before the duct tape swallowed his head.*

Carol wanted to put the jacket back in his closet, put it on permanent display in the Museum of Our Son, which meant I'd never see it again. But I had to insist we keep it out of the collection.

Our compromise was that we agreed never to wash it. I was looking at it just the other morning and I think I came across a few flecks of blood along the denim lapel of its collar. Brown by now. Have you tested the collar? Taken a DNA sample? Maybe you missed that bit of blood. Who's to say it's his? What if it was somebody else's?

What if it belonged to the man who did this to him? What if there was a skirmish, a bit of fisticuffs between them before his jacket was yanked off?

What if Billy got in one good punch?

I remember when Carol first bought Billy that jacket.

We're talking August here. A few weeks before his freshman year. Time to buy new clothes. Billy rolled his eyes over his mother insisting she cart him to the department store and help him pick out his clothes, but so it goes. She held onto the purse strings—tightly, I might add. Whatever threads Billy wanted to wear had to get Carol's approval first. And these negotiations were never easy. Not with her. Billy hemmed and hawed over each of her choices. Lacoste vs. Wrangler. Izod vs. Guess. Those two never saw eye-to-eye when it came to clothes. Carol was gearing him up for his first day of Sunday school, which was never going to fly with Billy.

This jacket, though… My God. The moment Billy laid eyes on it, it was over. That's it. Nothing else mattered. Billy begged. Outright begged Carol to buy it for him.

From the way she tells it, there were tears in his eyes. It was rare for Billy to take a stand like that, but he wouldn't take no for answer—so Carol caved.

He wore that new jacket on the first day of school. And the next. He wouldn't take it off. Indoors, outdoors. Freezing weather or sweltering humid heat. It didn't matter to him. The denim was so rigid, stiff as cardboard, before the sleeves eventually softened over his body. Took on his shape. Became a part of him. A second skin.

By the time his jacket came back to us, documented as evidence and subsequently lost for a couple years before popping up in the police department's basement, it was almost like getting him back. A part of him. His skin…

I can't tell you much about the shirt he had been wearing

that night. I think—I think it was blue? Baby blue? Or green… This is what I know about it, from what I read in the coroner's report: The neckline had been yanked so hard, the collar had stretched beyond its normal proportions. The neckline was gone. Loose and flimsy.

One of the sleeves was torn along the hem. I could hear it. That tear. I can always hear his shirt ripping. Duct tape peeling away from the spool.

But his jacket was still him. Still his shape. Still his smell. I was holding it just this morning, exploring the contours of his chest, his shoulders, searching the pockets one more time, just once more, just in case something was in there that we didn't find the first time, the tenth time, the fiftieth.

Billy had taken a Sharpie marker and scribbled the names of his favorite rock bands along the back. Names that meant nothing to me at the time, but now I've become acquainted with them. Doing my fair share of research by listening.

Carol had been downright apoplectic when she first saw all the different names along the shoulder, the sleeves— Black Sabbath. Dio. KISS.

But now they are code. Now they are an incantation. Words I can recite in his name, in hopes of invoking his spirit.

Carol had demanded Billy wash those names out. She hadn't agreed to purchase Billy this jacket just so he could deface it. If he wanted to wear his denim second skin to school, he better march to the washing machine and put it on rinse.

The permanent marker may have faded after a couple of washes, but the names persisted. The faint trace of the bands lingered along the sleeves, refusing to disappear. Like tattoos.

I had my fair share of ink. When Billy was just a little thing, he'd always get caught up in my eagle, globe and anchor. Just a little reminder of my Marine years.

Semper Fi.

Nothing but faded blue lines now, wrapping around my arm like ivy overtaking a statue.

First time he found the ink on my forearm, he traced his finger along the lower fluke of the anchor—still firm then. His finger dived down deep into my skin. Whether my tattoos served as the inspiration to decorate his jacket, I'll never know, but I'd like to think it was something we shared, regardless of agreeing with his choice in music. It's all noise to me. But these are the songs that Billy liked to listen to, slipping his headphones on and disappearing from his parents. Band names would mysteriously reappear across his jacket every couple weeks, once Carol had calmed down. As if she wouldn't notice their return. They shifted around the denim, finding new spots to pop up, the collar or the sleeves or a different corner along the back, magically rearranging themselves. For the life of me, I would have sworn Mötley Crüe had been scrawled along the lower left arm, not the right. But there it is. Every time I look the names over, studying his jacket, it's as if the bands have shuffled themselves in the middle of the night just to confuse me. They're never the same…

But the collar. Right. I called about the collar. I was studying the collar when I could've sworn I came upon a few brown flecks. They looked like rust, the very same corroded color of the sign standing over the strip mall they built on the vacant lot where Billy was found. But it must be blood. Has to be. I'd never noticed it before. Could the police have missed it, too? Could you tell the detective that I—

The dial tone buzzes in my ear.

I don't hang up right away. I let the receiver purr for a moment longer, like a flatline on an EEG monitor. Somebody's heart just stopped beating.

I didn't know Carol was listening.

"You've been eavesdropping on me?" I ask. "You spying on me, too?"

"It's not eavesdropping if you're yammering loud enough to hear through the walls."

"You should've said something. Must've thought I was whispering sweet nothings to my mistress down at the police station."

"*You*? With another lady?" Carol huffs. "That'd be the day."

"You saying you don't think I could have a little squeeze on the side?"

"That is *exactly* what I'm saying."

"Says you! I'm a catch!"

"You're already caught," she says. "Hook, line and stinker." Carol takes the phone out of my hand, gently placing it back on the receiver. "Let's go to bed, hon…"

I am a rite of passage for the police department.

Putting up with me. Humoring me. *Like a broken record,* Carol always says. For forty years, always with the same litany: *Anything new with the Partridge case?*

Anything new?

Anything?

There's nothing new.

Not under this sun.

Everybody—from the cops to Carol—keeps insisting all the stories have already been told. All the scenes have been written. Every word has been spoken.

So why bother? Why not just give up?

"There's nothing new on the case, Mr. Partridge," each and every officer has recited to me, over and over again. Years and years of the same line.

Sometimes I press harder. "But what about—"

"If we find anything out, believe me, you'll be the first person we call."

"But what—"

"You're gonna have to forgive me, but we got other cases that need attending to. Have a good evening, Mr. Partridge. Take care of yourself. Get some sleep."

I have a responsibility to my son. It's my God-given duty to remind them. Remind everyone in this town. The police. The man who did this to my boy.

Never let them forget.

Billy was here.

Billy is gone.

Billy was my responsibility and I failed him.

Maybe tomorrow I'll remember something else. Some other detail that slipped my mind. Some scrap of information just waiting for me to uncover.

I'll call back in the morning.

WRITE WHAT YOU KNOW

Rule number one: *Write what you know.*

More words of wisdom from our sage workshop instructor. "I don't want to read another story about vampires or wizards or Martians," he said. "I want to read about your life. Your experience. *You.*"

Brooke Jennings had some novel on the shelves about ten years back. Can't say I read it. From the sounds of it, I'm not alone on that one.

Fall from the Tightrope. Carol checked it out from the library. She left it in the living room for me to stumble on. Damn thing sat on the coffee table for weeks.

Now it's on her nightstand, relegated to the guest room. Out of sight. I don't think the book's been opened since it made its way into our house. It'll be due back at the library before much longer.

"Still waiting for my book report," I rib her.

"Nobody's stopping you from giving it a whirl," she snaps back.

"Come on. Just give me the CliffsNotes."

"You're the one taking a class with him," she shrugs. "I figured you'd want to read it. Get a feel for your new teacher."

He comes from Paterson. Grew up here. Guess he's got that going for him. Still has family around these parts, though I can't say I've ever crossed paths with any Jennings.

The Courier did an interview with him, heralding his ostentatious return. *Big Time Author Comes Back to His Podunk Hometown to Teach Illiterates the Craft of Creative Writing*. He's come back home after a stint living in New York. Big deal.

They quote him saying he's here to do research for a new book he's cooking up—"*I'm outlining a new novel right now," Jennings said. "I don't feel comfortable saying what it's about just yet, but I believe Paterson will serve as the backdrop for a story about real characters, facing real day-to-day dramas…*"

Anyone worth their salt can read between the lines on that one.

He's licking his wounds.

Probably got divorced. Or just washed up. Nobody moves back to Paterson.

Until I saw his author photo, swear to God, I thought Brooke Jennings was a woman. All this time, I pictured some earth goddess fawning over the lot of us while we all read our poems to each other. I sneaked a peak at the book jacket on *Tightrope* and—what do we have here—turns out Brooke Jennings is a he after all.

His novel sounded awful.

He who is without talent should cast the first critique, I know. But skimming the synopsis on the back of the book, I'm not going to lie… it made me want to read the damn thing even less. Something about a circus. A love triangle between an acrobat, the ringleader and some behind-the-scenes tent-hand.

I was hoping Carol would've read it. Tell me all the good parts, if there were any, just so I could act like I knew what the hell I was talking about.

No dice. The book popped back up in the living room, with a Post-It this time.

One word: RETURN.

Carol and I have communicated through sticky notes for years. We'll leave slips of paper for each other around the house. Footnotes to notes. Addendums to memories. Post-Its stuck to Post-Its, braids of paper stuck to one another.

I found a new Post-It stuck to the hallway wall. It's in my handwriting, I know that much, but I don't remember writing it. Its yellow edge flickered as a stray draft slipped through the hall, sending a shiver across the dozen different pieces of paper.

Memories of Billy cling to the house. Each bit of information jogs my mind. A space on the wall means there's a space in my memory, which I'm determined to fill.

Here's another Post-It: *Billy. Blue crayon on the wall. 1979.*

And another: *Billy. Sticker on table. 1982?*

I spent almost an hour in the front hallway alone, taking a step for every recollection I read along the wall. I'd put a foot forward, stop and glance at what I had remembered happening right there, translating my handwriting as best I could.

The whole house is covered in them. It's as if the wallpaper has begun to peel, shredding off into yellow flecks.

Billy. Photo w/ grandmother. 1983.

Doorframe. Measured height. 1976-1987.

Knick in wall. Baseball bat. 1981.

Time thickens here in our house. The air is dense with the past tense. I was taking a tour of Billy's life, following him around the house, reading a map.

Here was the closet where his baseball equipment is kept… This way to the kitchen where Billy had broken his mother's favorite vase…

The Post-Its flickered in the wind as I walked by. The hallways were encrusted in a yellow coral. I'm exploring the wreck of my own house, buried under a seabed of notations.

There were doubles. Sometimes two sticky notes stuck together for the same detail. The older one curled into itself, ink fading, while the most recent note was less decipherable, the letters uneven and rippled, as if I was losing my grip on my own handwriting.

No memory in the house has gone unnoted. Except for me. It appears that I'm the only thing under this roof that doesn't have a sticky note slapped on it.

I've almost forgotten about myself.

Write what you know.

Easy for you to say.

—

The Huguenot Public Library is a cinderblock shoebox crammed full of Danielle Steel paperbacks.

Back when Billy was a kid, Carol would bring him in nearly once a week. Those two had a deal—Billy could pick any three books he wanted. She'd check them out, no questions asked. Once he was done reading, Carol would bring him back to check out three more. Simple as that. She never laid down any law over what he could check out. If the kid wanted to plow through a Tom Clancy novel, fine. Why the hell not? *Happy trails...* If he wanted a Stephen King book to give him nightmares all through the 3rd grade, that was his call.

As long as he was reading, Carol left the decisions all up to him.

Only catch? She wanted a book report.

He'd hem and haw about it, but you could tell he

didn't mind. I'd hear the two of them at the breakfast table, chattering on about this or that book.

Billy just devoured books. I'd never get the titles. Just snippets of stories. Phantom tollbooths or magical wardrobes or precious rings that made you invisible.

Never could get a word in edge-wise once Billy's book report began. He'd barely come up to breathe in between sentences, just spilling these books back out at Carol, as if he were reading them out loud to her. Somehow, that boy could remember practically every plot point, every character detail, from whatever book he'd just put down, no matter how many pages ago.

Sounded that way, at least. To me, anyway.

Carol cut him loose, finally getting him his own library card. Laminated and everything. Now there was no holding him back. He'd ride his bike to the library. He read just about every book they had by the time he was in grade school.

Another year or two and he would've cleaned the place out. There wouldn't have been a book left under that roof he hadn't checked out at least twice.

I always wondered if the librarians kept a record. Who checked out what. Maybe there's an index card with Billy's name on it, listing off all the books he read.

I tried taking notice of the flow of novels rolling through our house, stashed in his backpack like contraband. I'd catch glimpses of their covers. Cellophane wrapped over their book jackets. Titles that may as well have been Russian.

A Confederacy of Dunces. On the Road. Something called *Siddhartha.* What were these books even about? Which ones were his favorite?

Did he have a favorite?

Carol fanned those flames from the moment he could crack open a book. It became something special for the two of them. Something only they shared.

Something outside of me.

I'm not resentful about it. I'm not jealous, I swear. Reading was never for me. So it goes. That's my cross. But the more and more Carol got him reading, the more they had their own secret language. Just the two of them. Their own little book club.

I never went into the library. That was all theirs.

Until now.

Entering the building, I wondered if I could pick out any of Billy's books. Maybe I could remember a couple covers. Ask the young librarian behind the desk where I could find this *Siddhartha.* See what that one's all about.

I'm not saying I'd read any of them.

Just curious is all.

What was the last book he'd checked out? Did it ever get returned? Do we still have it at the house? Is there an outstanding fine for it? Forty years later, I'm imagining we'd owe a pretty hefty sum. Ten cents a day for... what? 14,6000 days?

The hush that hung over this place, let me tell you. Libraries are no joke. It was deadly quiet in there.

Mausoleum-silent. Just the dull hum of fluorescents over my head and that's about it.

The plastic sign on the door says BOARDROOM. That's a stretch. Taped to it was a sheet of paper. Somebody had written WORKSHOP across it in magic marker.

This must be the place.

For community events, the library offers up this cramped backroom. No windows. The walls are eclipsed by cardboard boxes filled with books nobody checks out anymore. They're sagging on top of themselves. Look like stomachs to me. I couldn't help but think about dressing a deer, puncturing the intestinal lining and having all these dog-eared paperbacks come spilling out across your feet.

Some folks are already sitting at the boardroom table. Nobody's saying anything to each other. Feels so stilted. Is this an AA meeting waiting to get started? Been to plenty of those. *Hello, my name is Glenn and I'm an author…*

Seven rolly chairs. I'm one of the last to arrive, so of course, I've got to pick the one that's missing a wheel.

The fluorescents overhead couldn't illuminate the room as much as cast this dull, pearly sheen over everything.

One of the fiberglass tiles in the ceiling has dislodged itself, exposing the internal workings of wires and air-conditioning ducts. Something up there had sprung a leak. Been dribbling down for years now, from the looks of it. A brown stain has been slowly spreading across the fiberglass tile in the far corner, expanding over the ceiling like a storm cloud. The tile is sagging now.

Glancing around at the rest of the group, I see there's a good thirty years between me and most of these folks. Just kids. A couple housewives with nothing better to do than lounge around the library's conference room on a Thursday night.

What've they got to write about?

What in the hell do they know?

I spot a couple high school kids giggling together. One's on her phone, tapping away. The other spins in her rolly chair.

Sarah Midland sits across from me. Frumpy thing. Billy and his friends used to call her *The Cat Lady,* all on account of the pack of wild tabbies roaming around her single-story clapboard. She's lived in Patterson as far back as I can remember. Spent a fortune on canned tuna. She'll pop the lids on half a dozen tins at a time, leaving them on her front porch for all the feral felines to slink in and start eating.

Back when I was working, during the summer, I'd drive by her house with the window rolled down and I swear I could smell the fish drifting through the air. Spotted dozens of cats lazing around her roof, overwhelming the surrounding trees. Staring indifferently at the people passing by. Bet Sarah's got one hell of a story to tell. Can't wait for that whopper, whatever it'll be. She's wearing a pastel pink sweatshirt with a faded photo-decal of herself and a calico, smiling for the picture.

It strikes me that I might be the only gentleman in the group. Are there no other men here? *Jesus*, I think, *Carol's signed me up for a goddamn sewing circle.*

My skin feels loose, like it's sliding down to one side. Geez Louise, this is getting embarrassing. The hell has Carol done to me?

Siobhan Hanover sits next to me. She's a little more dressed up than the rest of us. The bracelets around her wrist keep slinking up and down her forearm. Pearl earrings. Can't say I know much about her. Husband's a lawyer. No kids, I don't think. They're living in this new McMansion back in Pinewood Acres—or Greenfield Cove or something like that. Can't remember exactly. The developers leveled about 150 acres' worth of woodlands just to make way for their pristine subdivision.

Billy and his friends used to traipse through those woods when they were kids. The amount of forest back there stretched along for miles. It'd be easy enough to get lost in there. Billy sure did. Once. When he was ten. He'd gone out there with a couple of friends. When dinner rolled around and he still hadn't come back home, Carol got on the phone with a few of the other mothers. No sign of him over at Alan Reynolds' house. No word from him at Walter Thompson's place.

Dusk was upon us. The woods were already pretty dark. The sun wouldn't reach through that dense canopy of trees for much longer, so I went out with a flashlight and combed through the woods. Called out his name every few steps.

Took me forty-five minutes to find him.

He was huddled into himself, leaning against a tree. Shivering from the cold. I had to carry him out of there. In the dark. He buried his face in the nape of my neck, desperate for whatever warmth he could squeeze out of me.

He whispered into my neck what happened. Turns out he and his pals went into the woods to play a little game of hide-and-seek. When it was Billy's turn to be *it*, he leaned his head against a tree, closing his eyes and counting to a hundred.

By the time he turned back around, he found himself facing the woods. All alone. *Ready or not, here I come*, echoing through the trees.

What Billy didn't realize—and why would he, really—was everybody else had run home. Didn't stop Billy from playing, though. Searching for his friends.

Come out, come out, wherever you are...

I could've killed those kids. Swear to Christ, I could've stormed straight up to any one of those boys and wrapped my hands around their throats and strangled—

"Good evening, everybody." Brooke Jennings enters the boardroom with a hefty exhale. "Nobody's ever claimed authors are punctual people, now, have they?"

He seats himself at the head of the table. Plops down a stack of books.

His novel. One copy for each of us. *Christ*. This SOB can't give them away. His own goddamn novel.

His hair's thinning up top. Not much weight on him. He wears a tweed jacket. All he's missing are elbow pads. *This guy can't be for real*, I think.

I shouldn't be here. I'm about a breath away from standing up and making a break for it, only for Jennings to start in on his pre-rehearsed spiel.

"Inside each one of you is a story that you've got to tell so badly," he says, "it burns. The longer it's bottled up within you, the more it'll gnaw away at your insides. That's the story I want to read. That's the story you're here to write."

All I've got are minutes. Little pockets of time that don't add up to much.

7:30 to 8:15.

8:45 to ten-past nine.

Then nothing.

Nothing at all.

Not until 6:13 the next morning.

Billy kept begging his mom to let him go to the fall dance. Carol didn't want him going. We both knew he wasn't going to cut a rug, but I didn't see the harm in it.

The boy was fifteen. All his friends would be there. He deserved a little fun.

As long as you're back by ten, I had said.

Billy begged for eleven. Outright begged.

Fine, I relented. *Eleven. Don't make me come down there and drag you home…*

Then we jump forward in time.

Hours slip by. Black holes in Billy's last night, unaccounted for.

The police found his body in a vacant lot less than five miles away from our front door. It had been drizzling off and on throughout the night, so his clothes were damp. The denim of his jean jacket was now a darker hue, deep blue, soaking wet.

No—not wet. What's the word?

Moist. His jacket was *moist* from the all the rain.

"A lot of you have probably never written anything longer than a few pages," Jennings says. I hadn't realized he was still talking. "Perhaps you have. Show of hands: How many budding novelists are there amongst us?"

Sarah Midland thinks about lifting her hand, then hesitates.

Only Siobhan Hanover raises her hand. Keeps it in the air a little too long for my tastes, like some goodie two-shoes looking to impress our teacher.

"That's great," Jennings says in a way that makes me think he doesn't believe it's that great. "We are going to unlock those stories bottled up within you. We're going to get them out. Exorcise them, once and for all."

The capillaries in Billy's right eye had hemorrhaged,

the coroner's report said. Three of his teeth had folded in—two upper central incisors, one lower lateral.

"I want you all to know," Jennings continues, "I'm not your 'teacher.' There are no grades. No pop quizzes. This is about you finding your voice. Think of me as your base coach. I will guide your story to home plate. We will pull that story out of you, kicking and screaming, until it's ready to be shared with the rest of the world…"

Billy's lower jaw fractured at the hinge.

A collapsed nasal cavity.

All this, just waiting under the duct tape. A present you never want to unwrap.

One last look at my son.

"So…" Jennings glances around the table, taking us all in with a rakish grin, as if this were the beginning of some goddamn swashbuckler. "Who's got a story to tell?"

GRAY GHOST

There is a boy in our house.

Sleep isn't coming easy for me. Not after the workshop. I had this dream—a new one—about Billy.

He's ten years old tonight. Sitting on my chest. The weight of him puts a real pinch on my lungs. He's peering down at me, grinning as if this were all a game to him—while I'm struggling to breathe. My lungs just can't reach any oxygen.

When I woke, I could still feel that heaviness against my chest. Coughing like a cropduster engine hacking to life. My breath wasn't coming back fast enough. Kept spitting up these gray ropes of phlegm. Desperate for some air.

The weight eventually dissipated.

Billy was gone.

Carol still sleeps downstairs in the guest room. If

she'd been here with me, I might have knocked her out of bed with all my flailing about.

Small mercies.

We tried sharing the bed downstairs for a spell, but Carol kicked me right on out. A few too many nights of my tossing and turning was enough for her.

"Out," Carol demanded. "For the love of Christ, go back upstairs."

"Never bothered you before," I said. A bit stung, I'll admit.

"I'm a light sleeper," she answered.

"Since when?"

"Since I can't move anymore! All I do is lie here, on my back, while you're doing somersaults… I can't sleep like that."

"I'll stay in one place, I promise."

"Just go upstairs," she pleaded. "To our bed. One of us should, at least."

"Are you sure?"

"I'll be back up before you know it." The way she said it made me realize she believed she'd never climb up those steps to our bedroom again.

"You're gonna get lonely down here without me," I said.

"Believe me, I get my fill… There's plenty of you around this house."

That meant the second floor was all mine now.

The boy, too. Billy's room is down the hall from ours. I had been banned from entering for years. I wonder if she realized she was relinquishing her responsibilities to me. Now that she's trapped downstairs, I'd have Billy's room all to myself. To clean and curate. Give guided tours. *Welcome to the Museum of Our Son…*

We'll start with Billy's dresser. Here you'll find artifacts of his childhood, particularly in his teenage years. His cassette collection marks a shift in his musical tastes between ages eleven and thirteen. Out with Cat Stevens, in with the heavy metal.

You'll notice his posters focused on music as well. A few movie posters. We have Ralph Bashki's Wizards. A couple covers torn from his comic books. He had a strong predilection for fantasy and sci-fi, as you can see by the art pinned to the wall.

The clock on my nightstand table said it was two-thirty. The numbers seethed in angry red digits. I climbed out of bed and headed for the bathroom. I was in the hall, my hand on the bathroom door, when I saw the boy.

His gray face had a duct tape complexion.

He could've been ten. Maybe older. There were no discernable features. I couldn't guess what age he was, exactly. Just the cold gray slope of his silvery skin.

Where were his hands?

He was standing in the doorway to Billy's room. The door was only open by a crack. There were no lights on. Not in his room or in the hall. Shadows in shadows.

But his face. His gray face glowed like a dull moon.

His eyes were nothing but black circles. Wobbly magic marker. The lines were crooked, contorted like a pair of warped eggs wobbling in the air. The longer I looked at them, stared into them, going down deep, the more they seemed to spin.

Every time the boy exhaled, his trapped breath bulged out in places about his head. Not just around his mouth, or where I imagined his mouth would be.

But his ears. His forehead. Around the nose.

His gray face. His black eyes. His expanding, pulsing dull silver skin.

He was staring at me.

"…Billy?" I said his name out loud and immediately regretted it.

Giving my fear a name, like that.

My son's name.

The boy stepped back inside his room and sealed the door behind him.

Click.

"Glenn?" It's Carol calling from downstairs. I must've woken her. "That you?"

"Yeah."

"Who are you talking to?"

"Just myself," I lie. "Go back to bed."

SCRAPBOOKING

"**W**hat's your story about?" The tone was rhetorical, but I could tell Jennings was aiming his question my way. "If you can't answer that for yourself, sometimes it's smart to start at the end and work your way backward."

Easy for him to say. That's always been my problem.

I've never had an ending.

Just false leads. A string of inconclusive details that go nowhere.

Dead ends. That's all I've got.

There were rumors of a vicious bike gang descending upon Paterson in the middle of the night. Their Harleys rolled through town and found Billy walking home, alone, whisking him off the side of the road like a hawk plucking up its prey. They performed some Satanic ritual in the vacant lot, sacrificing our son.

Or the ol' chestnut about Billy falling victim to a serial killer working his way up the Eastern seaboard, one town at a time. When this mystery man spied Billy hitching by the side of the road, his killer instincts prickled and he picked up my son.

Rumors. Wild stories. I followed them all until they fizzled out. Drug dealers. Alien abductions. Shell-shocked soldiers turned vagabonds drifting from town to town. No tale is too absurd to give a spin. To believe, even for just a moment.

Not one of them has the right ending. They peter out before reaching the good part.

There's no closure. There are facts I still haven't found. Minutes that haven't been accounted for. Who's responsible for compiling them?

Every last detective who has handled Billy's case over the years has either died or retired. Nobody holds onto the case for that long. *Hot potato, hot potato...*

It's a regular roll call of cops. Over forty years of Paterson's finest.

Let's see—there was Detective Payne, for starters. Good guy. Really tried cracking it. He held onto the case the longest. Had a heart attack about twenty years back, so detective Chaplin inherited it from him.

Chaplin juggled it for about ten years before punching his time clock for the last time, so Chaplin handed it over to Detective Matthews.

Matthews couldn't be bothered to solve it. He stashed the file in his desk drawer and promptly forgot my son for five years. He tossed the case to Detective Linda Corrigan, where it's been since January. We'll see if she bucks the trend.

I'm doubting it.

Corrigan had been loaned to Dade County by the State Bureau of Investigation. Looked to me like she was in her forties. Not much of a smiler. Not that she had much of an occasion to grin around me. *Just the facts, ma'am.*

Our conversations have always been stilted.

"Anything new?" I'll ask.

Always ask.

"If there was, Mr. Partridge, I would tell you." Her impression of a patient person could use some work. I can always hear how aggravated she is with me.

"What about that—that eye-witness account I called you about? The girl who saw him leaving the dance? Did you talk to her yet?"

"We did, as a matter of fact. Detective Payne interviewed her. She told him everything she knew twenty-five years ago."

"Maybe she forgot something," I suggest.

"I appreciate your help on this, Mr. Partridge." Like hell she does. "But I'm going to need to ask you to stop calling Mrs. Coughlin. She's told us everything she could remember. If you keep calling her, she'll file a complaint. Against you."

"You got any kids, Detective?"

A pause. "No, Mr. Partridge."

"No. I reckon not."

I get the feeling she doesn't like me. Has no patience for my help. She won't say much, but she thinks I'm meddling. I can read between the lines.

Carol agrees. "Let the woman do her job, for Pete's sake. Stop hounding her."

"Don't you think I've let her do her job for long enough? Don't you think it's high time somebody actually *did* something to find out who did this? To our son?"

"Don't get on your high horse with me, Perry Mason…"

"I don't care who figures it out," my voice lifts. "It could be the mailman for all I care. I just want answers! I want these people to do their goddamn job!"

"So let them," Carol snaps back. "Let them do their job and stop bothering them all the time!"

There's a stack of cardboard boxes collecting dust in the basement at the Dade County Sheriff's Department, filled with beginnings for my book.

Not one ending.

On the front of each box is Billy's name: PARTRIDGE, WILLIAM—just so they'll know where to stuff whatever intel I send their way and promptly forget.

Write it off.

I'm the only one keeping this case alive. Used to be that I'd wake up in the middle of the night, thinking of something I wanted to ask Detective Corrigan.

But by the time morning came around, I would've forgotten it.

So I started taking notes.

Whenever I bolted up in bed, I'd reach for the nearest Post-It pad and scribble down a detail. Some clue the police might've missed. I'm not knocking the Dade County Sheriff's Department—not all of them, at least—but there have been times when it was evident that these guys weren't giving my son's case their all.

Me—all I've got is this case.

I'm no gumshoe. I'm not solving my son's murder.

I'm just trying to tell his story.

I want to reach *The End.*

Thanks to my creative writing workshop, I'm starting to get a better idea of what that means.

I need an arc. Rising action. Falling action. Climax. A protagonist.

Antagonist.

I'm taking notes all the time now. You never know when inspiration is going to hit. Billy's beginning to mix in with grocery lists: *Milk. Eggs. Billy's first baby-step.*

My pockets are always stockpiled with scraps of paper. Carol has to empty them out whenever she does laundry, pay stubs and napkins raining over the floor.

"You need a better filing system than this," she tells me.

"Did I just hear you volunteer to take dictation?"

"Not on your life."

By the time I turned sixty-five, I had a pretty keen suspicion my memories were starting to unfasten. Items around the house were suddenly disappearing. I'd confuse the names of friends with one another. So I began to catalogue Billy's life. I'd incessantly write down the details into a notepad that I keep tucked into my pocket.

It was the simple things at first. The easy memories. I mapped out Billy's entire week, a page for each day. No slip of information could've been too trivial to write down, well aware of how tenuous my memory would inevitably become.

I grappled with details no one is ever expected to remember. I had the sinking feeling this was just the beginning. The notion of what's to come...

A sinkhole was slowly forming.

A cavern was hollowing out underneath my mind, the ground collapsing onto itself, until there was nothing left supporting my memories.

Through the years, I've poured his life into over a half dozen notebooks.

I've got a hobby. A way to pass the time. But in my cataloging, I sensed my desperation. My need to know that I remembered these things, actually *knew* them, no matter how trivial. What started as a way to remember details was becoming a meandering biography, documenting all of Billy before he vanished.

When the time finally came that I wouldn't be able

to account for him—he'd still be here. On the page. I thought I could read over his life, approaching him with fresh eyes, like opening a new book and reading his life story.

Looking through the notebooks now, I can see my handwriting begin to loosen through the pages. Started off as a tight, concise script. The pen laced my words together in an efficient cursive, keeping my sentences neat and close. It filled up a page with over a hundred thoughts. But the deeper I read my own words, I noticed the handwriting start to slacken. The words sprawl farther out than before. A single sentence stretches on for twice the amount of space it would've a month ago. Sometimes passages pop up twice, echoing old ideas further into the notepad.

On some pages, I don't even recognize my own handwriting.

Who in the hell wrote that?

The scrapbook came in handy. It was one of those rinky-dink three-ring photo albums you buy at the pharmacy. Nothing special. Burgundy leatherette cover with gold stamping. Fifty sheets of fast-stick magnetic pages, clear plastic overlay that self-adheres to the page. Seals your picture in place.

Carol had started it before Billy was born. *The Book of Billy* it says on the cover in black rub-on letters.

The first picture was a printout of his sonogram, nothing but a blurry image of this tadpole swimming about.

We added snapshots of us at the hospital. Bringing Billy home. His birth certificate is sealed under the cellophane sleeve.

We added extra sheets whenever we needed more space. Just pop open the binder and slip in a refill. Every memory of Billy is preserved within its pages, like a butterfly collection, every scrap of his life pinned in place, framed and dried.

But the pictures peter out once Billy reached his fifteenth birthday.

No more photos. No more ticket stubs. No more of his drawings from school.

Now it's newspaper clippings.

The pages are overtaken with yellowing articles, their headlines blaring— *Local Boy's Body Found in Vacant Lot. Ten Years Later and Still No Clues in Boy's Death. Murder in Small Town Lingers.*

Our local paper did a report on Billy when he was first murdered, covering it for the crime blotter. Hack job, if you ask me. Nothing but static facts. They reprinted his yearbook picture—Billy hated that picture—next to a photo of the vacant lot where they found his body. A strip of police tape stretches across the gravel drive.

They interviewed me for the article, but they got what I said all wrong.

"There's a special realm in hell for the man who murdered my boy," Glenn Partridge, William's father, said. "If the judge won't send him there, you bet I will."

I said it. I'm not denying that. I just didn't think they'd print it.

That's not how I want to tell my son's story.

Every couple of years, it's the same ol' song. Some wet-behind-the-ears intern will ring me up and ask if I'd like to do a follow-up.

I oblige, of course.

All press is good press, right? What does this cranky old coot got to lose now? Maybe I can kick up some dust. Jog a few memories from the folks around here.

These fresh-faced rookies always toss out the same questions. Poor cubs don't know what to do with me. I could do the interview for them all by myself.

I end up rehashing the same canned answers, every time. I may as well write up a press release. Send that in to the paper instead. Save us all some time.

We go through the motions of the same interview.

Q: *How does it feel after all these years, not knowing?*
A: *You never truly get used to this sort of thing; but life goes on.*

Numb. That's how it feels.

A dull cold deep in the marrow, radiating through my bones. There's frost in my lungs. It's a chemical chill, like breathing Freon. My throat burns from it.

I've lived in this not-knowing for so long now, I don't know anything else anymore. I don't know what else to feel. There's nothing, nothing left for me.

Q: *Is there something you'd like to say to the person responsible for your son's death? Do you think they are still out there?*

A: *All my wife and I are asking for at this point is closure. Please, if you could come forward and let us understand why, why Billy, why it had to be our son... then we can move on with our lives. That's all we want... To move on. Don't we deserve that?*

You took our son.

Our only light.

You used a sort of brute force reserved for animals. Vicious animals.

Not only did you destroy our son's life in the most heinous way, but you quashed ours as well. What life have we lived since you took him?

With no sense of remorse, no sense of dignity or compassion, you have let my wife and I live our lives without any light, without hope.

We have nothing now.

Nothing.

Do you see us in town? Do you pass us on the street? Have you ever felt the compulsion to speak to us? To let us die in peace? With dignity?

We are empty now. We are hollow people.

You have gotten older, too. Maybe you have a family now. Children of your own. Grandchildren, even. That's something we will never have.

What that must feel like. *Grandchildren.* To have

your own life extend through generations, your family expanding beyond the reach of yourself…

We'll never know that. Never experience that love.

Our family tree was cut down before it could branch out any further.

Did he call out for his mother that night? Did he fight back?

What did he do to you to deserve such a terrible death?

What did he ever do to you?

Why him?

Why?

Q: *Can you forgive the person that did this to your son?*

A: *The bible asks us to forgive others their trespasses. Forgive, and you will be forgiven. I want to believe we could find the strength to live by Christ's teachings.*

This is where I feel like my imagination has really taken flight. I've found inspiration in tortures of all types. Stuff that would make the Marquis de Sade blush.

Sometimes I even surprise myself.

What would I do if I had an hour alone with this gentleman? In a room with no windows?

A trip to the local hardware store is an opportunity to research. Every tool feeds my fantasies. A ball peen hammer could flatten out his bare feet like a pair of raw hamburger patties. I could pluck his fingernails out with pliers. It's just a matter of getting a good grip around the end of the nail and yank. There's that initial *crack* of the nail breaking free, followed by a tender tear of flesh, like duct tape peeling off the spool. I could sprinkle a little lye over his legs. Let it settle there for a spell. Let it eat away at his skin. Let him smell it, the chemical burn filling up his nostrils. Take a whiff of his own flesh and know that was him, melting.

And if I was in a real pinch, I could reach under our own kitchen sink, pull out the bottle of bleach under there, and pour a thimble full in each of his eyes.

Or the real cherry on top…

I could just pull out the duct tape. A whole new roll. I could bring it up to his ear and peel off a strip, *slowly*, so it makes that high-pitched squeal, like fabric tearing. I'd start at his ear, sealing it up with the beginning-end of the strip and unwinding the roll across the back of his head, wrapping it around his other ear and around his eyes and around his nose and finishing the first loop around the entire hemisphere of his head before looping around once more, this time just a fraction higher, to cover more of his hair, more of his skin—*'round and 'round and 'round it goes, where it stops, nobody knows*—until his eyes are buried below and his nose is pinched and his mouth is sealed shut, mummifying the man in a metallic bandage, until there's nothing left to see, nothing left for him to say, to plead, to breathe.

Revenge is a young man's game. I don't have the stomach for it anymore.

In my forties, I wanted nothing but vengeance. Retribution by my own hands. I wanted to string him up and strangle the life out of him. Watch the light fade from their eyes. There was a lot of drinking back then, so most of those years were a blur.

But my anger got me nothing.

In my fifties, I wanted justice. I wanted the man responsible for my son's death brought before the law so they could cast God's judgement upon him. I cleaned myself up, made my vows to get my act together. For Carol's sake. For Billy. I focused that rage. Found righteousness in my wrath. Channeled it into the law.

But the law got me nothing.

In my sixties, I wanted the truth. I wanted Billy's story told for all to hear. To know what happened to my boy and that it never happen again.

But the truth got me nothing.

I'm seventy-seven now.

I'm tired.

I just want it to be over. All of it. I can barely even pick up a ball peen hammer anymore. Can't lift it over my head, no matter how motivated I may be to smash that man's teeth in. My body won't let me get revenge, even if I wanted it.

There's no justice. There has never been justice. The guilty go free. The innocent suffer. The wicked live. This story goes on unfinished, untold.

It never ends. It will never end.

No one should live this long, feeling this way. Living with this anger. There are times when I believe my rage is the only thing keeping me alive. What's left?

I just want to close the book now. Finish it.

The end.

Is that too much to ask?

Don't look at the back of the scrapbook. There's a lot of loose notes that I'm going to give to Detective Corrigan when I get around to it. I still need to organize them. Receipts with details scribbled on the back. Pages ripped out from other books with facts written in the margins. Post-Its. Magazine subscription slips. Used envelopes. Phone bills. Matchbook covers. Ticket stubs.

Anything with a blank space has become mine for the writing.

It's all here. All of him.

If you read it all, every last scrap, his face comes into view. Who he is now.

What he's become.

What do *you* see? Can you see him?

My son?

TWO BIRDS

There's an extra setting at the dinner table.

Carol sets three plates out every night. I'm not allowed to mention it. I just have to let her. That's our unspoken arrangement. However we want to remember him, honor him, we can. Neither of us is allowed to step in and take that away from each other, no matter what.

A deal's a deal.

I can't take Billy's chair. I have to grab another from the dining room, usually mine, and place it in the bathtub. It'll ruin the finish before long, for sure, but it's the only piece of furniture in the house that fits through the bathroom door.

Carol's arms won't reach much higher than her waist these days. That means the scrubbing's up to me now. I help her into the tub, one leg at a time, sitting her down in the chair before climbing in myself.

"Get ready for some company." I seal the shower curtain behind us.

"Just don't get fresh, mister."

"You rebuking my advances?"

"If you know what's good for you, you'll keep those hands where I can see them."

"Just wait till these magic fingers get to work, *mademoiselle*," I say, straining. "You'll be begging me to keep it up."

She's trying hard not to smile. "Get those hands cracking, Romeo. Let's see what those fingers are made of."

At first, I tried bathing her while kneeling next to the tub. Most of me ended up getting wet anyhow.

This way, we both get clean. *Two birds, one stone.* She works the soap into a lather, then hands it off to me to clean all the hard-to-reach spots.

Washing her hair always brings back Billy.

"Keep your eyes closed, hon. Don't want the shampoo stinging you…" I say it to her, but I catch myself saying it like I'm saying the words to him. The tone is too tender for Carol. We never talk that way to each other. Not anymore. She knows who I'm talking to, she has to know, but she lets me say it that way, anyhow.

She lets me talk to him.

He's three years old now. All covered in suds. He's slapping the tiny icebergs of bubbles bobbing along the water's surface. He brings his hand up, discovering the soapy bubbles settled into his palm and clapping his hands together until they burst into the air, like dandelion seeds scattering everywhere. I'll catch them.

Billy glances up to me, this look of wonder on his face.

To see the world through your child's eyes. To discover the magic in our lives. Something as simple as taking a bath becomes a miracle. There is nothing but joy in Billy's eyes and it fills me, overwhelms me, until I feel like I might drown.

"How'd you and Mom meet?" Billy had asked me, much later. This was back when he was about seven, I believe. Eight or nine, maybe. It's hard to pinpoint the exact year anymore.

It was back when love was still something he had to look forward to.

"By balloon," I said. I loved telling this story. Billy loved hearing me tell it.

My signature yarn.

Carol always acted like she couldn't stand it, always rolling her eyes and making a fuss—while I'd spy a smirk play across her lips. "Don't get your father started," she'd say, always listening in. Just to hear me tell the story all over again.

The first day of Miss Carter's fifth grade English class, we were all given a notecard. Each student wrote their name and address in thick magic marker, taking our time to spell as legibly as our handwriting allowed. One by one, we lined up in front of Miss

Carter's desk. Waited our turn to have the top corner of our notecard stamped by her hole-puncher. At the edge of her desk was a wicker basket full of balloons. We each picked out our favorite color, choosing from blue, pink, green.

I took a red one.

Miss Carter asked us not to blow them up yet. She insisted we keep our balloons empty until everyone had their cards punched. She handed out a piece of string to each of us. Instructed us to tie one end through the slit in our notecard. She went around the room just to make sure everyone's knot was tight.

In a single-file line, the class followed Miss Carter outside to the basketball court. There was an air tank of helium out there that looked like a missile dropped out from a B-52 bomber. She filled up our balloons, one by one, tying them off so they wouldn't sputter away. It was up to us to attach our string to the balloon. I had to hold mine under my armpit, so it wouldn't slip off.

Once everybody's balloon was full, Miss Carter counted down—*One… two… three!*—and the class all let go of their notecards. I tried to follow mine for as long as I could, squinting my eyes the higher it lifted.

Back in the classroom, Miss Carter pulled out a map of the county. She pointed out where we were. She took a box of thumb tacks from her desk, saying that if any one of us ever got a letter in the mail from somebody who found our notecard, we should bring it to school and share. For every letter, she'd take a thumb tack and pin it to the map over the location of the return address. The pin was the same color as our balloon, so that we'd know whose was whose.

Thumb tacks scattered over that map fast, the entire state pockmarked in pins. Pen pals popped up from as far away as Sellers, South Carolina.

"Glenn?" Carol calls out. "You still back there?"

I'd come home from school every day, making my way to our mailbox. I'd open it up in hopes of finding a letter addressed to me.

Weeks went by and nothing. Nothing ever came. The lucky students read their letters to the rest of the class. Everybody else had a pen pal but me, it seemed. I imagined my balloon must've hit a wind drift—blown out over the ocean, some sea turtle thinking it was a jellyfish and eating it, choking on our correspondence.

The school year went by and—nothing. Nothing ever came. Not for me.

I would look at that map, pockmarked in pins. I'd think to myself that I'd never have myself a pen pal. Fifth grade finally came to a close, all of us kids slipping into the summer. Ended up forgetting about the whole thing anyway.

"Glenn? Where'd you go?"

And then, one day, I think in August, my mother asked me to go get our mail. I reached my hand into the box, only to pull out a letter with my name written in chicken scratch.

Turned out to be a letter from your mother. She had found my balloon in the field right behind her house. She decided to try writing me back. Not at first, mind you. She sat on it for a while. Debating whether to reply or not. Took her sweet time.

Until… well, until here we are. I've loved her ever since.

If your mother had never written me back…

Where would we be now?

"Glenn… I'm getting cold."

I come back to the tub.

To our bodies.

The slope of Carol's back is before me, the skin sagging off her shoulder blades. The water has lost its warmth. I can't say I know how long we've been sitting here. We've both pruned up. Then again, our skin was pretty wrinkled to begin with.

"Glenn," she pleads. "I'm so cold…"

WRITING PROMPT

"**A**nything new on the Partridge case?" There's no hope in the question at this point. Even I can hear it.

I'm begging. *Anything new?*

Anything?

"Can't say there is, Mr. Partridge," the voice on the other end says, full of false pity. "I'll make a note for Detective Corrigan you called. Should I have her ring you?"

"No," I say.

"You sure about that? Wouldn't be a problem at all." Whoever this officer is, he's sure having a hard time pretending to sympathize. He's mocking me.

"No, thank you."

"You have yourself a good night, Mr. Partridge. Take care, now…"

I hang up before he does. I don't want to hear the

dial tone. I can't bear to have it reach into my ear, vibrate through my spine.

I can't sleep.

Billy's bedroom has always been off-limits to me. *I shouldn't be in here,* I say to myself as I cross through the threshold, like I'm stepping over the red velvet rope barricading spectators from an exhibition.

Carol would kill me if she found me in the Museum of Our Son. But sleep isn't coming anytime soon. It never comes now.

I pick up his pillow. The lingering hints of his shampoo have faded by now. I still bring it to my nose and take in a deep breath, hoping to inhale the faintest trace.

Nothing.

Just as I put the pillow back, exactly like I found it, I hesitate.

There. Right there.

I catch another memory. Just like that, it washes over...

Carol and I tiptoed into Billy's room after he lost his first baby tooth. The root had been softening all week before he finally tugged it free. He came running into the kitchen—*Mommy, mommy, a tooth, I lost a tooth!* He had the biggest gap in his gums when he smiled. Carol made such a big show of the tooth fairy. She planted the milk tooth under his pillow and we all said our prayers—*Now I lay me down to sleep, I pray the lord my soul to keep, if I die before I wake, I pray the lord my soul to take.*

What a god-awful thing to pray for. To say. Who asks for such a thing?

I want to take it back. Take the prayer away.

We had to wait until Billy was fast asleep before we could sneak back in. Carol extracted the milk tooth while it was up to me to slip in the nickel under his pillow. My hand made its way under his head. I was about to pull out when, glancing down, I saw Billy's eyes were wide open. He was staring right at me.

Shit. I froze, caught red-handed. *Shit, shit.*

Carol had already eased back into the shadows without drawing Billy's attention. *Shit, shit, shit.* Billy sat up, rubbed his eyes, finding my hand on his brand new shiny nickel—"What are you doing, Daddy?"

From that night on, I was a thief. *The Tooth Bandit.* Never lived that one down.

I place the pillow back. I even try pressing a dent in the center, molding an impression of Billy's head, as if he was just resting it there, only moments ago.

I think back to the coroner's report. The medical examiner had scribbled a note about how Billy had suffered repeated blows to his face.

Blunt force trauma, it read.

Crushed his septum. Pushed back his lateral incisors until they snapped at the root. Three teeth altogether—two upper central incisors, one lower lateral.

I'm picturing his teeth sealed up inside some evidence bag, zip-locked and stashed away. Ain't no way the tooth fairy is going to flutter through the Dade County Police Department, head down into the basement and sift through all the cardboard boxes marked PARTRIDGE, WILLIAM, just to find a few broken teeth.

They will go unclaimed. Unpaid. The tooth fairy owes my boy fifteen cents.

My teeth are all long gone by now. They started falling out a few years back, so I went to the dentist to have the leftovers yanked out, finishing what time had started. Replaced them all with dentures. I got nothing but gums now.

Would Billy even recognize me? This elderly shell that's replaced his father? Look at these dwindling muscles. The wrinkled skin. Liver spots. Receding hairline.

What would he think of me now? His room is such a mystery to me. I hadn't realized how long it had been since I last set foot in here. Might as well take the tour. Take him in.

Billy loved collecting Hot Wheels as a kid. I find that shoebox in his closet, some miniature junkyard full of die-cast metal replicas. I picked one up.

A '67 Chevelle SS 396.

Spitting image of Walt Thompson's car. All the way down to the body work.

The Madeira Maroon hardtop. Black bucket seats.

Walt's been working as a forklift driver down at the box-making plant for the last twenty-five years.

He's gearing up to retire soon. Lives with his wife in the same single-story frame house he grew up in, no more than a ten-minute drive from here.

They got a couple kids, all grown up. Kids of their own.

Walt's a granddad now.

They were teenagers at the time.

Just kids.

Walt showed up at the wake, along with Alan Reynolds. Even signed the guest book. Can't say I saw either of them there—but sure enough, their signatures are buried amongst the rest.

I looked. Double-checked, just to be sure. Sure enough, Walt paid his respects along with everybody else in this goddamn town.

You got to ask yourself: *Who could do something like this?*

You look at everyone around you, wondering: *What if it was them? What if they were the one's that did it?*

For years, *for forty years*, like a broken record: *Why our son? What did Billy do to deserve this? Who could have done this to him?*

I always keep a pad of Post-It notes in my pajamas pocket. I pull it out and scribble down a reminder for myself to call Detective Corrigan in the morning.

I write it in the dark, so it was barely legible: *Chevelle. Walt Thompson?*

Walt wasn't a friend. Alan Reynolds wasn't a

friend. Always picking on Billy when they were kids. Pushing him around. Billy had the bruises to prove it.

Taunting him. Teasing him.

I won't let go of the car. I keep turning it around in my fingers, like I'm giving this Hot Wheels its state inspection. Examining the chassis. The brakes. The tires.

I try crushing it, squeezing the toy in my hand, like my fist is some junkyard shredder. My fingers have enough force to pop the windshield. The car emits this high-pitched squeal, metal rending as I tighten my grip. The headlights blow next, one followed by another—*Pop! Pop!* I just keep squeezing it. Crushing Walt's prized car into a compact cube of steel ready for smelting, forgotten by all.

When I release my fingers, one by one, I notice the side mirrors have left marks in my skin.

But there it is. This swell in my chest. The sensation spreads through the rest of me.

A hunch.

Walt Thompson. Alan Reynolds.

Walt's '67 Chevelle.

'67 Chevelle.

—

"Dade County Sheriff's Department."

"Yes, I think I might have some important information in the Partridge case."

"Two calls in one night, Mr. Partridge. We're going for a new record here." The voice on the other end of the line doesn't seem too pleased. Whatever sarcasm was in his voice before has dissipated, replaced with something a little more irked.

"I wonder if anyone searched Walt Thompson's car for possible traces—"

The voice on the other end cuts me off. "Just hold on a sec, Mr. Partridge."

So I hold on. I've been holding on for forty years.

"I don't think it's wise to point fingers like this," the voice suggests, trying to sound a little too nonchalant for my tastes. "I'll have Detective Corrigan reach out… but if I were you, I'd take a breath and think about making any hefty accusations."

"Maybe if you boys did your job, I wouldn't have to do it for you."

The line goes silent.

I decide to keep going. On a roll now, why stop? "Did you search Walt Thompson's car?"

"Mr. Partridge…"

"Did you?"

"I'm not at liberty to share that information—"

"Who am I speaking to?"

"You want to speak to my superior?" He's no longer hiding his disdain.

Walt Thompson and his friends were no secret. Alan Reynolds and Johnny Mannefort were always at his heels, following him around like a pair of diligent puppies. Always racing through the streets in his car. Knocking over mailboxes on a Saturday night. Drinking in his Chevelle. Wreaking havoc in our town.

Everybody knew about Walt and his pals. We all had our own story. Cats tied to tree branches by their tails. Out comes the baseball bat. *Kitty piñata,* they called it.

Bricks through windows. Beer cans in the ditches.

These secrets always remained out in the open and nobody even batted an eye. These boys were our boys, Paterson's flesh and blood. So we deal with them.

Tolerate them. Keep them close and hope nobody gets hurt.

There were never any arrests. Those boys never went to trial for any of the petty crimes they committed over the years. Vandalism. Theft. Arson. On and on.

Boys will be boys, their parents said. These are the boys the police protected?

What about Billy? Didn't he deserve protection, too?

Boys being boys. No harm in that, right? Just a little harmless fun on a Friday night. Those boys had been tried in the eyes of Paterson and found innocent, where they walk free, where they live and breathe, amongst their families, their children and now their grandchildren—because sometimes the law can't convict.

Sometimes justice must be done by a higher court. Forgive me if I'm a little impatient for St. Peter to make up his goddamn mind.

Everybody knows what those boys had done. Everybody talks. Just not to me. This small town of ours, where everybody's in everyone else's business. The rumor mill just cranks away, doesn't it? Saying *this* and *that*. Never saying what matters.

And still, *still*, the police aren't willing to lift a finger. *Lack of evidence.*

Lack of proof.

"I want his teeth," I say into the phone.

"Come again?" It's not what this cop was expecting me to say. I didn't expect it myself, truth told. "I want his teeth back."

"Mr. Partridge, I don't—"

"I'm supposed to give him fifteen cents. I owe him fifteen cents. Billy always blames me for taking his tooth fairy money and now I've got to pony up."

There's a stretch of silence from the other end of the line. Finally, the voice says, "You have yourself a good evening, Mr. Partridge. Maybe think twice before picking up the phone next time, okay?"

I don't respond.

"And another thing, Mr. Partridge? Leave Walt alone. For your own sake, okay? That man's done nothing to you, so don't drag him and his family into this."

Drag his family.

Into this.

WRITER'S BLOCK

A book isn't written, our sage writing instructor suggested. *It's rewritten.*

I'm beginning to believe him.

Just when I think I'm done with one chapter, I'll remember something else. Some scrap of information that I let slip comes flittering back. I've got to catch it before it disappears for good. I got to go back into the book and fix it before I forget.

It's constantly changing. *The Book of Billy.* Growing up on its own.

Revision, revision, revision, as they say.

Books are like babies, right? Isn't that what authors always call their novels? It's important to put him down on paper. Watch him walk on his own two feet.

"Getting a book published is like seeing your kid off on his first day of school," Jennings regaled our workshop, reliving his glory days on the shelves.

Carol stood with Billy at the bus stop on his first day to school. Me, I had to work. You think I wouldn't trade in that day to've been there?

I'm not holding out any hope of my book getting published. He's just for me. My eyes only. I lost him once, I'm not about to let go of him again.

"So when do I get to read your magnum opus?" Carol asks.

"When I'm finished."

"Any idea when that's gonna be?"

"When it's done."

"You're no fun," she mutters.

Carol's never stepped into the hardware store and locked onto a roll of duct tape, imagining the blood seeping up from the crevices. Whenever someone tears off a piece of tape, she doesn't hear Billy's voice buried beneath it, wrestling for breath.

That's been for me to deal with.

Nobody else.

But I'm wrestling with the story. It's getting away from me. Taking on a life of his own. The timeline contorts and I scrap it all. Memories don't meld anymore.

I need a new scrapbook.

The first album is all full now. Pages don't fit. I can't cram anymore in. The magnetic cellophane sheets have given away to reams of paper. Now that I'm writing, committing Billy to the page, I need to build an addition. I can't force it all into one album anymore. There's too much. It's getting too heavy for me to lift.

My boy's too heavy for me.

—

God have mercy on us all, we're workshopping each other's stories in class now.

Siobhan reads first. I'm going on record and saying I don't get it. Sorry, that's the God's honest truth. I've got zero idea what her story is supposed to be about.

We start with a married couple, that much I know. Their relationship's on the rocks. *Okay. With you so far.* Then, one morning, out of the blue, they find a package on their front doorstep. No return address. *Fine. So it goes.* Inside the package is a video cassette. Just a blank VHS tape. It's a recording of them. Somebody's been filming them from a distance. Not my cup of tea, but I can still follow along.

So this couple keeps getting these videos. A new one every morning. For a whole week, this goes on. Rather than call the cops, they watch them—and see themselves as other people see them. Unhappy. Empty. Whatever.

So this couple. At first, they're terrified of these videos. Like somebody's stalking them or what have you. They're always looking over their shoulders, wondering if somebody's recording them right now. Then the husband gets the idea that they should make a show out of it. Get back to who they used to be when they were first married. Buy each other flowers, dance around the house, make a big splash over how happy they are, how much they love each other. *Let 'em record that.*

They go about this grand production, making romantic candlelight dinners, toasting each other, slow dancing in the living room... on and on. They even retreat upstairs to the bedroom. Leave the lights on as they... You know. *On with the show.*

The next morning, when the husband opens the front door to get the newspaper—no video. The recordings stop, just like that.

Now that this couple is happy again, there's nothing to record.

The end.

Jennings goes gaga over it. Makes sense. "Very Raymond Carver," he crows. Whatever that means. He's been mollycoddling Siobhan from the get-go. Those two have their own secret literary language, steeped with authors the rest of us have never heard of. Siobhan's always chatting him up during our smoke break. Asks him about whether he's read this book or that book. If he had a chance to pick up the new Marukami novel. Read this week's *New Yorker*. It never ends with her.

I don't need to be Jennings' favorite. What burns me is that the cabal with Siobhan has made the rest of us feel like we're amateurs. Blowing sunshine up that manicured ass. Jennings even promises to introduce her to his agent. Share Siobhan's story with him "once it's polished."

Siobhan's basking in it. Soaking up the adulation like she's sitting in a tanning booth. She's all leather-skinned by now. A Gucci-clad cow chewing on her own cud.

Jennings finally gets around to the rest of the group. After fifteen minutes of fawning all over Siobhan's story, he asks, "So what did you guys think?"

Siobhan's beaming. Nothing can break her. She's as pristine as the gold earrings pulling her ear lobes down. Don't think I didn't notice the color of her lipstick deepening itself tonight. Those red lips of hers are practically bleeding.

"Glenn?"

Takes me a moment to realize Jennings has called on me. I turn, a bit taken aback, unsure what I'm supposed to say.

"Siobhan's story? What'd you think?"

"It was nice."

Jennings isn't going to let me off the hook. "Can you open up your critique a bit more for us? What did you think was *nice* about it?"

"What you said sounded pretty spot on to me."

"Come on, now," Jennings keeps wheedling me. "Don't be shy. I know this might be a little out of your comfort range, but we're here to offer feedback. It's helpful to each of us to hear what others think."

Siobhan's smile slips. Not a lot. Just a bit. I can see she begs to differ with Jennings, but she's not going to second guess our gilded workshop instructor.

"I don't know," I say after thinking about it. "Felt a little, you know. Fruity."

Siobhan looks at me. What she sees doesn't impress her.

"Not fruity," I back-pedal. "Just, I mean… Why'd the couple start doing all that stuff in front of the windows? They must've known they'd be seen. They knew whoever was making these videos would see them. Wasn't like they were actually doing it because they wanted to. Wasn't because they loved each other… Right?"

Siobhan's cheeks seethe just so. That ain't her makeup. "They're being held hostage in their own home."

"Fine. But then they're off the hook the second they put on a show of it? What's that say about their relationship?"

"It's not a show." The hoity-toity vibe has chipped away.

Sarah Midland blushes, easing back in their rolly chair. The high school girls have clearly clocked out, weeks ago. They busy themselves twisting in their chairs like they can't keep still for more than five minutes. Incessantly smacking their gum, sounding like the *clack clack* of a typewriter, *click-clacking* away.

Siobhan lays into me. "The recordings are

a *metaphor*. The tapes are an expression of their relationship. They've lost themselves, but they find a way *back* to each other. That's not something I think you'd understand."

"Okay," Jennings finally steps in. He's losing the reins on his own workshop. "I think that's good for now—"

"I just don't get it," I shrug. "Sorry. Cleary, I'm in the minority here."

"No," Siobhan agrees. "I don't suspect you would *get it.*"

"Thank you, Siobhan," Jennings veers into the conversation. He's got nothing. "She brings up a good point, though, Glenn. How's the writing been going so far?"

"Fine and dandy."

"Care to share with the group next week?"

"That's all right."

"It's your money. You can do whatever you want. But… it's not really a writing workshop if you don't share your writing, which isn't fair to the rest of us."

"I will. Soon. Promise."

"What's slowing you down?"

"Just got a…" What's this guy's problem? "Guess I got a little writer's block."

Siobhan huffs. It's just under her breath, but the boardroom is hushed enough for the slightest sound to travel.

"Writer's block is a myth," Jennings announces. "Writer's block happens when you refuse to let your story tell itself the way it wants to be told. If you feel like you're suffering from writer's block, then you're not listening to your own story."

Now I'm being chastised.

Peachy.

"Mind if I give you an assignment?" he asks me.

"I got homework now?"

"Just an exercise. Nothing too difficult. Next time you sit down to write, I want you to work on your sense memories."

"Memories?"

"Think of a moment. Just a single moment. Cooking eggs or polishing your shoes or brushing your teeth. I want you to write out the whole scene with your senses. What do you smell; what do you taste? All five. Think you can do that?"

"Yeah," I say, not sounding so sure of myself. "Sure, I can do that."

"Really paint the scene for me, okay? See if that can't help push you through… And then bring something in to share with the rest of the class. Next week?"

I glance at Siobhan from across the table. I can tell she's already sharpening her knives, ready to carve into my story up like a goddamn Thanksgiving turkey.

"Sure," I answer back. "Next week."

PARTIAL PRINT

The police lifted a partial print thirty years back. Not enough comparison points to make a match. The core and delta points were lost. Not enough minutia.

But there it was. The bifurcating ridges of someone's thumb.

It came off the duct tape. The person who wrapped the roll around Billy's head had to press his thumb against the tape to peel it off. That print ended up embedding itself in the shell's innermost layer, preserved within the acrylate polymer, like a fossilized footprint of some dinosaur.

Billy loved dinosaurs as a kid he knew more about dinosaurs than I thought was possible always talking about tyrannosaurus rex pterosaurs ichthyosaurus—

The impression environment was uncontrolled, I was told, thanks to Billy's breath. When he was suffocating, he kept exhaling against the adhesive, thereby creating enough humidity to soften the print from its original impression.

The ridges loosened. Just enough to render any possible match inconclusive.

His thumb.

His thumb.

I'm thinking of this Christmas ornament Billy made back in kindergarten. A thumb-print reindeer. Just paint your thumb with a little bit of acrylic and press it against a glass bulb ornament. Let the print dry. Then take a Sharpie marker (*they drew a pair of eyes over his eyes those haunting eyes empty and blank staring back*) and draw your eyes, your nose, your mouth and your antlers—and there you have it.

Eight tiny reindeer ready for the tree.

Carol added a dab of her red nail polish for Rudolph. Billy hung them up along with the rest of our ornaments. His tiny fingerprints dangled from our tree.

If a partial print doesn't have the core or delta structures, any matching methods based on alignment are going to fail. Singular structures won't correspond. There's no one-to-one.

No bullseye.

No match.

This was '87. You could forgive forensics for not being up to snuff just yet. But Detective Finland told me the thumbprint was a dead end. It just wasn't enough.

Thirty-five percent. That's all there was.

Thirty-five percent of this man's thumb. A jury would need more. They'd need to compare the width of the ridges. The distance between oil pores. Where do the ridges end? Where do they bifurcate? Where do they change direction?

Three to sixteen points of comparison.

How many did we need?

Detective Finland had Xeroxed the print. He blew the thumb up until the image was the size of an unripe watermelon. He was big on visual aids. The ridges and contours looked more like a nautical chart for some convoluted tributary in the Amazon or something. Once you're in, there's no navigating your way out.

I asked for a copy.

For my scrapbook.

Finland wouldn't miss a duplicate, so he printed me off an extra copy and promptly forgot about it.

This is why I miss Detective Finland. He never asked any questions. Never asked me why. *Why do you want that, Glenn? Why are you doing this to yourself?*

"Don't tell me I never got you anything," he muttered to me when he handed it over. "Merry Christmas."

He didn't need to know. Probably didn't want to. It's better that way. Not knowing. *Ignorance is bliss* and all that.

Me—I want to know everything.

Need to know.

I broke one of the ornaments five years after Billy's death. The first time Carol and I decided to try and make merry again, celebrate the holidays and all that.

We should've waited. We weren't ready.

I wasn't ready. Not yet.

I'd picked up a tree. Some rinky-dink thing. The runt of the whole lot. Didn't cost much. The smell of pine filled the car as I drove home. Needles falling all over the footwell. Carol pulled out the ornaments from the attic and we got to hanging.

"Need help?" I asked.

This used to be Billy's thing. Helping her decorate the tree.

"Sure," she said. She tried on a smile and it didn't fit, so she took it away.

"You tell me which ornament you want and I'll grab it."

"It doesn't matter."

I was trying. Really trying. Hell, we both were.

But it didn't feel right.

None of this felt right.

There was a drink in my hand. I don't recall what. Something brown. Peaty. That left me with my left hand. I reached into the Christmas box and pulled out the first ornament my fingers came upon. I don't even think I was looking at it.

"How about this one…"

Turned out to be one of the glass bulbs. I brought the ornament up and got a good look at it, before realizing what it was—I noticed Billy's fingerprints with the burning red acrylic nose and ended up crushing the bulb right there in my hand.

Something about holding it. Feeling the bulb in my palm. Seeing the whorls and ridges of Billy's fingerprint. My reflexes suddenly kicked in and I squeezed.

The bulb was mirrored glass. Really thin stuff. Fragile.

It shattered so quickly.

All the king's horses and all the king's men…

Blood rose from between my knuckles and dribbled to the floor as the glass chewed into my skin. It felt so warm. This red swell in my fist.

Carol yelled at me. "*What* are you *doing*?"

I destroyed a precious artifact. This precious, priceless, irreplaceable piece of evidence of our boy. I might as well have stormed into the Museum of Our Son and stomped on his belongings, tearing his posters down, one by one.

I was the destroyer of memories. The annihilator of keepsakes.

Now we only have seven reindeer.

Rudolph wouldn't make it back.

Billy's fingerprints have been in short order nowadays. There's no getting them back. What lingering traces of his touch remain in our house have been slowly wiped away. But for years, *years*, it was impossible not to look at our house on some microscopic level and know his fingerprints were everywhere. On everything.

What had he touched? Which cartons? Which boxes? Should Carol keep them? Should she dust the house for prints, until the negative space of his fingers was everywhere, the walls and banisters and knobs, looking like tiny bacteria teeming about the house?

How long before they would be gone? Shed like skin from our house, never coming back. Replaced with other finger prints.

Luckily, I had our friend's thumbprint to focus on. His print interested me more. The Xerox ended up in the scrapbook. It's easy to get lost in it. I'd stare at the swirling riverbeds, working my way through that labyrinth of eddies and ridges.

I made a copy of the copy. Who am I kidding? I've made more than one.

Lost count by now.

Twelve. Let's just say a dozen for the hell of it. Round it up. I've made twenty copies of this thumb. Thirty. For research purposes. I took a pencil and maneuvered through, like the thumb print was a game to play. A maze.

Billy loved mazes. He could spend hours tearing through one of those puzzle books. Best present Carol ever got him. One of those collections of brain busters. Give that kid a pencil and he'd sprawl out on the floor and lose himself for days.

But this maze was rigged.

I found my way in somewhere around the lower delta and following the pathway up toward a radial loop in the center. But as soon as I was there, I funneled through a whorl and hit a dead end. I had to backtrack where I'd begun, all those arches ago. Even then, though, I couldn't retrace my steps.

There was no way out of this mystery man's thumbprint. I was trapped. There was nowhere to go but forward, forging ahead through this tangle of ridges, like I was heading upriver on some endless journey.

Billy told me about a book he read once. *Heart of Darkness.* "Sometimes you remind me of this guy," he'd said. "Kurtz."

I didn't know what he meant by it back then. Was that a good thing? I didn't ask. Wasn't until I checked the book out of the library that I even tried reading it. But the book is all Greek to me. Talk about a slog of a novel. It's thin, but every sentence is so dense, I get lost in the words before I reach a punctuation mark. Those periods are life rafts. I'm clinging for dear life after flailing about the page, gasping for air.

Who the hell is this Kurtz fela? The hell is he going on about, anyhow?

"What're you working on?"

Carol catches me poring through the pages of the scrapbook. I try not to do this around her. It's my hobby, not hers, but now I feel like I've got to hide it.

"Nothing." I've been adding a few new chapters,

editing them down if they don't fit Billy's timeline: *Who was the last person to see him leave the dance? Was he with anybody? Who did he talk to while he was there?*

"You're spending an awful lot of time on that scrapbook, hon," she says.

"Is there something else I should be doing with myself?"

"What about a different hobby?"

"Like what? Bird-watching? Stamp collecting? Ship in a bottle?"

"I'm just worried you're losing yourself in… in…"

Our son?

"…your project."

I'm tired of being told what I need to do with myself.

I'm tired.

"I can always get a different hobby," I snap. "Another son? Never get one of those again."

SUBMISSION

I bring Billy into my writing workshop.

You're supposed to print copies of your pages for everyone else in the class so they can make notes in the margins.

But my margins are already spoken for. No blank spaces left.

The spine barely holds itself together. The burgundy cover is belted by a couple rubber bands, loose pages curling into themselves.

Jennings stares at the scrapbook and I swear I see his face go pale. His eyes never leave the photo album, unable to look away from it.

"What is this..." He manages to ask, but the question mark wilts.

"This is my son."

GRAY SHADOW

There's a ghost in my lungs.

Even before the doctor points to the tumor, I spot its gray shadow drifting about my ribcage. That ghastly plasma hovers in the upper corner of my left lung, nothing but a blurry mass spreading its metastasized silhouette across my heart.

"Do you smoke?" The doctor asks, reminding me he's even in the room.

"Used to. Pack and a half of Newports in my prime, but not any longer."

He nods. Somehow, he doesn't seem satisfied with my answer. He's young. Much too young to be mouthing off about *endobronchial bronchogenic carcinoma*.

Around Billy's age, from the looks of him. Handsome lad. Clean cut. Maybe they knew each other. Maybe they even went to school together.

"How long since you quit?"

"Last pack had to be about… oh, ten years ago now? Maybe I've had an occasional slip, but nothing serious. Scout's honor."

"I see." He takes a quick breath. "You're from the area, yes?"

"Born and raised."

I'll die here, too—which, from the looks of my chest X-ray, won't be too far off.

"Work around here?"

"Thirty-five years in the Wellington Manufacturing Plant."

Down the drain.

"Doing what?"

"Corrugating cardboard all day, every day. Maybe you've seen my work?"

He smiles. Humoring me. "So you were on the assembly line?"

"Yes sir."

"Breathing in some hefty fumes, I bet…"

"Every damn day." I gave thirty-five years to that factory. What did it give back? A pension that barely keeps the electricity on. I lorded over the same machine for decades, pulling a lever that corrugated pulp. Stamping ribs into countless thousands of boxes. *Millions*, I reckon. Reams of stiff paper that will end up holding some family's books. Or food. Containers in waiting. I breathed in noxious chemicals until it weighed my chest down. Wasn't so surprising to wake before work and cough up blood, all the cardboard particles scraping at my windpipe.

Thirty-five years, come and gone. They put me out to pasture with a pat on the back. And what have I got to show for it now? What's left of me? My lungs are so stiff nowadays, they feel like cardboard flaps fanning out from my ribcage.

The doc's heard enough. He's ready to move on. "Next step is to schedule a CT scan. Based on what we see there, we'll make plans on where we go from there. But we'll want to perform a biopsy on that"—he points to the shadow—"right away."

Could Billy have been a doctor? I'm imagining this man, my doctor, is my son. They look alike. At least what I imagine he'd look like now, all grown up. After a haircut.

This could be Billy, couldn't it? Could he walk me through my checkup with the same clinical efficiency as this kid? Would he have been any warmer to his pop?

The hell are you doing, Glenn? I chastise myself. *This isn't your son.*

That's not Billy.

Doc notices and probably assumes it had to be his grim diagnosis that's got me turning beet red. He adjusts his bedside manner a bit. "From where the tumor is located, I'm guessing we'll end up doing a bronchoscopy. It's a tad less invasive."

"I don't like the sound of that…"

"It's better than some other alternatives, believe me. We'll send a tube down your throat to get a tissue sample. From there, we'll see what we're dealing with."

But I already know what it is. I can tell by the shape of the shadow. The contours of it. Where his eyes were. His mouth. The mole just under his right eyelid.

Billy's looking back at me from inside, like he was peering out a window.

That's my boy...

"If it's small-cell lung cancer, we've got our work cut out for us. It'll spread to other parts of the body if we don't treat it in time, so it's wise for us to move on this."

Time. How much longer before his shadow grows? Looking at the X-ray, I can't help but wonder if his ghost will spread throughout the rest of my body.

Will this gray boy take over my bones? Will the pleural effusion spill into the rest of my X-ray's negative space, filling up all the pockets in my body? Possessing me entirely?

I'd gladly give Billy my body, if it brought him back. *You can have me,* I wanted to say to the X-ray. *All of me. I'm yours, son...*

The only thing stopping me is the doc. "Does this make sense?"

"Think so."

"Any questions?"

"No, sir."

"I'm crossing my fingers for non-small-cell lung cancer," he says, focusing on the X-ray. "It's more common. Much more treatable. Regardless, it looks like we're still in the limited stage. It sure is a good thing you came in when you did."

"My wife gets all the credit."

"We should all be so lucky to have someone looking out for us, right?" He gives me a mock-conspiratorial grin, nudging me with his elbow.

"Says you," I huff. "She wouldn't let me hear the end of it till I scheduled an appointment."

"Well—better give your wife a hug and a kiss. She might've just nipped this in the bud before it could've gotten much, much worse."

"Don't tell her that," I say. "It'll go right to her head."

"You've got it."

"I'll tell her you're hiring, though. Maybe you can get her off my back. Have her bother some of your other patients for a change…"

This makes him laugh. "Do that. Please."

I glance back long enough to take Billy in, watching him drift throughout the image of my ribs, hiding from this man who wants to take him away from me.

"Any chance I could get a copy?"

—

Carol's stewing in the waiting room. She has a magazine resting in her lap, open to the same page she'd flipped to when the nurse first called me in.

"What'd he say?"

The look on her face. I can't tell if she's worried or hopeful. She'd insisted on coming with me. Probably didn't trust me enough to walk in through the sliding doors on my own. Like I'd skip my own checkup.

That meant hefting Carol out of bed. Unfolding the wheelchair from its collapsed position and plopping her in, pushing her all the way here.

"Just a bad chest cold," I say. "He says it could be nearing pneumonia, but he's not worried right now. I'm pushing through it."

"He really said that?"

"Got my prescription for antibiotics. *Take two and call me in the morning…*"

"*Hmm.*" She shakes her head, her face puckering. "I want to talk to him."

"Carol…"

"Just a couple questions."

"Sorry to disappoint you on your diagnosis," I say. "But the doctor signed off. I'm free to go."

"That's all he said? Case closed?"

"I'm fine. Just a bad cough. Happens to the best of us."

Silence from Carol.

"You can't get rid of me that easily," I say with a wink. "We're stuck with each other."

"Well," she grumbles. "I don't see why you won't let me just talk to the man."

"You're sore is all." I give her a peck on the cheek. "If it's any consolation, the doc wanted me to let you know he appreciates you stepping on his toes."

Pushing Carol out of the hospital, I'm now aware of the weight in my chest. The presence of something separate from me lingering within myself.

A ghost. A metastasizing specter.

A gray-and-silver shadow contrasting against that ghastly black of my lung. The negative image of my son settling into my chest, tethered together in pale veins.

Thatta boy, Billy…

Sometimes, it's the little things that leave a father feeling the most proud.

PAPERCUTS

Jennings makes sure to sit next to me tonight. I'm surprised he doesn't offer to hold my hand.

"So gang," he starts. Buoyantly, I might add. I've never heard his voice this high-pitched before. It doesn't last. He coughs lightly to clear his throat. "Tonight, we're workshopping Mr. Partridge's story… Everybody read the pages Glenn sent?"

I glance over at the Bobbsey Twins smacking their gum. The brunette meets my eyes, but doesn't stay on me for long, spinning around in her rolly chair.

Nobody's making eye contact with me. Everybody looks like a bunch of puppies who just piddled over the carpet.

"Good," Jennings breaks through the silence. "So this is how we're going to handle ourselves tonight. First half of the critique, we all give positive feedback. Let's each share what we liked about the story. Discuss what we thought worked."

Nobody pipes up. Not even a nod.

They won't look at me. None of them will look. Like they're afraid.

Of me.

"Then we'll discuss which areas we feel might need a little more love and attention. If a character doesn't ring true or... Let's all just offer up suggestions on how we think the material can be improved. Sound good?"

Ring true. Jennings tosses it out there as if that's his opinion, but he doesn't want to say it up front. He wants somebody else to say it first.

Ring true.

He turns and gives me this charity-case smile. From this close, I notice a shaving nick on his neck. I almost expect him to lean over and whisper in my ear—*We'll be gentle, don't you worry...*

"Ready, Glenn?"

I nod.

I'm not ready for this. I can feel my insides start to twist. *Stomach in knots,* is the way the saying goes— but my God, this feels worse. My intestines are coiling around my spine, a python weaving around its prey and squeezing the life out of it.

Jennings turns back to the group, takes a breath. "So who wants to begin?"

Pop goes the girl's bubble gum.

Sarah Midland ducks her chin into her chest. She's been bringing in her knitting during our workshop these last few weeks. Jennings actually had to ask her to stop. Too much of a distraction. *This is not a needle-point workshop*, he said.

My hands are buried below the table. I knead out the knots from each knuckle. The low wattage of fluorescents pulses just over my head. The brown stain in the ceiling tile has grown since the last time I sat here. Since last week, the water has seeped further into the neighboring tile.

"Anybody?" Jennings doubles down. "We're looking for words of encouragement here. Who's got something positive to say about the piece?"

Silence.

Siobhan Hanover gives a sharp intake of air. She leans forward, mouth open, ready to speak her mind. But nothing comes. The words just aren't there.

"Siobhan?"

She's caught. No backing out now. She takes a moment to adjust her seat. "I thought it was rather… *vivid*."

"Vivid," Jennings nods, relieved. *Finally. Now we're getting somewhere.* "Good. Think you can be a little more specific, Siobhan? What about it was so *vivid* to you?"

Pulling teeth. This is like pulling teeth.

I can feel my dentures loosen from my gums. This was a stupid idea. *Stupid.* I want to stand up and work my way around the table and grab back each photocopied stack of paper from their hands.

Jennings and I had agreed which biopsy of Billy's

life to examine. We selected one of the more legible sections. He helped with the copying. Slipped the scrapbook under the library's own photocopier and duplicated him. Now they all had him, facsimiles of him, ready to dissect and eviscerate and wheedle around his insides.

I want to take Billy back.

You can't have him, I want to shout. *Give him back to me. Give him back.*

I glance over at Jennings' copy. I can see there's ink spread across the front page. So much red ink. He's made notes in the margins. Underlined passages.

All that red. It's bleeding up from the paragraphs. Each sentence is slashed.

Billy's bleeding. *My boy is bleeding.*

"I—just don't feel comfortable critiquing this," Siobhan says. "I mean, is it even a short story? I thought the assignment was to write a story."

"It's my story," I say. I'm going to say more, but Jennings holds his hand up.

"I know this is your first time up to bat, Glenn. So let's just remember—no one's out to attack you. We're not here to hurt each other's feelings. This isn't about you, personally, okay? This is about your story. So I'm going to have to ask you to try and separate yourself from your writing. Do you think you can do that, Glenn?"

The tone on him. Treating me like a child. I want to slap that pandering grin right off his face.

To the rest of the group, he says, "We're here to

help foster Mr. Partridge's voice, so we need to focus our feedback on what's good for his story. Not our own."

Jennings turns back to Siobhan. She stiffens.

"Siobhan. You said *vivid*. That's a pretty powerful word. What particular passage did you feel that way about?"

Siobhan slinks back into her seat, shaking her head like she's just tasted something sour. She's recalling something, a sentence I wrote. "I'd rather not…"

"It's okay," Jennings offers.

Nobody else is willing to stick their neck out. Siobhan, poor Siobhan—she must brave the empty void, alone. Jennings, our hallowed workshop instructor, hotshot New York author, has cornered her. She squirms in her seat, the rolly chair pushing back from the table, stalling as best she can, but she's got to respond.

"The part about…" Her voice drifts. "About finding the boy. In the lot. When the police first—"

—come upon his crumpled body, his torso twisted, his chest resting against the ground while his waist was turned in the opposite direction, like a rag doll—

"—found him. That was a very difficult section for me to read."

"That's good," Jennings says. "That's good. Just remember to speak from your own perspective. How the work makes you feel."

"This isn't the type of story I'd personally choose

to read," Siobhan continues, emboldened by her own prim morality. "What's the value of it? What kind of person would want to read that? I'm sorry, I don't like that type of story. It's not for me."

I keep pinching my knuckles under the table. The arthritis is flaring up so much, I can barely squeeze my hand shut.

"That's fair," Jennings says. "Not everything has to be to our tastes. But wouldn't you say Glenn's writing is *evocative* enough to make you see these things?"

Siobhan looks mortified. Betrayed by her own guru. "I'm just offering my opinion," she retreats. "Don't we see this sort of thing in the news enough?"

Jennings looks around the room. "Did anybody else have a similar feeling? Did any of you feel like the writing was too explicit?"

I can tell Sarah wants to nod, but she's afraid. If she puts herself out there, Jennings will pounce and make her expound upon her kitty litter opinions.

Nobody is willing to come to Siobhan's rescue. She's all alone. Some sacrificial workshopper. Jennings has no choice but to return to her. Harp on her.

"Siobhan." His voice sounds dry, about to crack. "Would you say the explicitness is there to jolt the reader? Shock them out of their seat?"

Siobhan's mouth opens. She has something she wants to say that she hasn't voiced yet. I can see it now. The thought, simmering. It's there. Ready to share.

I know where this is all going. I know what she wants to say.

"But that's not what he's doing. This isn't fiction. He's not—"

"Now, now," Jennings admonishes her from breaking one of our workshopping cardinal rules. "Remember: *Critique the writing, not the writer.*"

"This isn't a story!"

There it is. She's said it.

Somebody finally said it.

"It's not, is it?" Siobhan turns to the rest of the group. To Sarah. To *anyone* but me. She's exhausted from the circuitous posturing of our workshop instructor as he struggles to drag something constructive out of all this, a crappy magician trying to pull a dead rabbit out of his hat. It suffocated inside.

Jennings is desperate to keep the workshop together. "What if we pivot…"

"She's right." This from Sarah. She's finally piped up. Her head is still bowed, but her eyes are alive now. "He's writing about… about him."

"This is my life," I say to Sarah.

To Siobhan.

To Jennings and the rest of the class.

To Carol.

To the room.

To the ceiling and the leak in the roof.

To the library.

To Detective Corrigan and the Dade County Sheriff's Department.

To the long list of detectives who abandoned my son.

To this goddamn town.

To every last citizen within the county line.

To the people who know the truth and have decided to hide it.

To Walt Thompson.

To Alan Reynolds.

To Johnny Mannefort.

To the people who did this to my boy.

"This is my life."

Jennings places a hand on my shoulder. "I know this is hard, Glenn. But it's best for you to—to just listen to what everybody's got to say. Don't feel like you need to defend your work. Every writer wants to, I know. Believe me, I've wanted to protect my words from the wolves *plenty* of times."

I want to give him my fists. Just lay into him. Telling me to back down. Aren't I supposed to protect my son? Isn't that what a father is supposed to do?

Bunch of wolves, alright. Circling around my boy. *Stay away from him.*

"But for now…" *Jesus, is this son of a bitch still talking?* "You have to let everybody say what they have to say. Take it with a grain of salt. Make sure you write it all down. And later, much later, when the dust settles and you've got some distance from tonight, you can decide for yourself whose feedback you agree with and whose you don't. Keep the feedback you need and scrap all the rest."

"You don't get it." It comes out of me much more forcefully than I expected.

Jennings winces, just a pinch around his eyes. I can tell he's disappointed in me. "That may be the case." The words come out slowly. Ooze out from his mouth. "But what if a few of us felt the same way? Do we all not 'get it?' Every reader is going to react differently, but think about what feedback keeps coming back to you. Where's the repetition in your reader's response? You need to listen to your—"

"But this is how it happened."

"What happened?" Jennings' diplomacy is straining. He's losing his patience.

"My story. This is how it happened."

"In real life, perhaps. But we're talking about your *story* here. We're trying to find spots that were confusing to us. That might need more attention. That's all."

Jennings raises his hand. "Show of hands. Who thought the piece was too explicit?" His hand remains in the air on its own for a beat before Siobhan joins it.

Then Sarah.

The high school girls aren't far behind. Before long, everybody but me has their hand up.

"You can't take this personally, Glenn," he says. "This is not about you, it's about your story."

Jesus, this guy. He doesn't know. Doesn't

understand. After all that he's seen, all he's read, he still believes this is something I've made up. "It's about Billy—"

"No matter what the source of your story is, once you commit it to paper, it becomes its own living, breathing entity. It's no longer your life. It's not a piece of your past or personal experience. It's fiction. It has to stand on its own two feet."

They're taking him away, I think. *These people are trying to take Billy from me.*

A million tiny papercuts carving him up.

He's bleeding out.

—

I waited for Jennings in the parking lot. The library's about to close, so a handful of folks are filing out now. It drizzled a bit. The asphalt glistens. It's not raining anymore, but I've been outside long enough to feel my clothes getting damp.

Moist. I'm feeling the moisture seep into my skin, working its way into my chest. If I wait out here much longer, I'll catch my death.

I spot a mother shepherding her three kids toward their car. Got a waddle to her. She's fed up with her children, scolding them as they run off into the lot.

"No running," she shouts, but they're not listening. "Watch out for cars!"

Suddenly, she realizes she's not alone—glancing

my way and halting. Something in her eyes seizes. She's just stopped in the lot. Looking at me funny.

Do we know each other?

She's in her forties, from the looks of it. Maybe a bit older. Her round cheeks remind me of bobbing for apples. One of her boys starts kicking somebody else's car.

"Leslie?" The name pops out of me, as if I plucked it from the ether.

Leslie Givens. No—not Givens. Not anymore.

It's Reynolds now.

"Mr. Partridge?"

She recognizes me. She's backing away. One step, now two. Her eyes haven't left mine. So wide. Her mouth remains open by a crack, but no words come out.

"Leslie…"

She breaks away. Her pace picks up as she slips into the maze of cars.

"Leslie!"

Leslie Reynolds. I'm rinsing away the last few years, seeing if I can get a better picture of how she looked when she was in high school. Those candy-apple cheeks, all polished. Her tightly curled hair sprouting out from around her temples.

I didn't recognize her. Looking so tired. Forty years steeped into her cheeks.

Leslie Givens.

It had been her, hadn't it? She still lives here. I

counted three kids. I pull out the Post-It notepad from my pocket and scribble down a note: *Leslie Givens. 3 kids. 2 boys, 1 girl. What had she told police? Call Corrigan & ask about her statement.*

The pad is moist from the drizzle. The words bleed into the yellow, losing their shape. But I can't forget this. This is important. This clue. *Don't forget. Hold on to it.*

Jennings finally makes his way into the parking lot.

I've been waiting by his battered sedan. Wasn't too hard to figure out which car is his, thanks to the box of novels sitting in the backseat. I spotted his author photo through the window, that black and white grin of his smiling back at me.

"This isn't a story." I say it too loudly, but still. It has to be said. For Billy's sake.

"Glenn," he says, voice spent. He must be tired. "Everything okay?"

"This happened. This is my life."

"I understand that. I truly do…"

"No, you don't—"

"Look, I think it's great that you're writing from what you know. But just because it happened to you doesn't mean it's inherently *dramatic*."

"What's that supposed to mean?"

He takes a deep breath. All he wants is to go home. To his parents' home. The basement. To his own work in progress. Is it the story he's dying to tell, I wonder?

"You told me to write about what I know," I press. "This is what I know."

"Real life doesn't necessarily equate to something other people want to read." He stares off into the lot. "An author's responsibility is to take their experiences and sculpt them into a dramatic narrative. You have to shape your history. Give it an arc. Structure it in such a way that real life might not offer."

I can feel my chest tighten. The gray ghost inside me shifts, resists.

"You want me to lie?"

"It's not lying. It's *storytelling*. You get the difference, right? What are the stakes? How do you raise them?"

"Raise the stakes?" I cough. It's a wet one. Billy's beating against my ribs. He's tearing through my lung tissue. He wants out. He wants to get away from this man.

I shouldn't be here. I shouldn't be in this workshop. Shouldn't have let Carol talk me into this. Shouldn't have tried it.

This is all wrong.

"I just want to put an end to all this," I say without realizing it. My body is shaking. I can't control myself. All the blood in my body rushes to my chest. I can feel it. I can't stop shaking. My cheeks are wet. When did I start crying?

I hear myself let out this—this sound. A moan. Is that me?

Jennings doesn't know what to do.

"I want it to be over with. I want to—" A coughing fit breaks out from inside me. A dizzy spell takes over. I need to steady myself. My hand reaches out, grabbing at air.

Jennings takes my arm, holding me up. "Easy. Easy, now…"

He takes this as a step in the right direction, I can tell. He gives me that smarmy smile of his. He thinks he's helping me. Progress.

"We're all looking for an ending," he says. "It's the hardest part of writing."

I'm about to say he doesn't understand. *Again.* He's not listening. Christ, how far is this guy's head up his own ass? I don't want to find an end to my story…

I want justice. I want the truth. I want revenge. I want the men who did this to pay. I want them to know what they've done to my family. To my wife. To our life.

I want them to suffer. I want them to spend every minute out of what remains of their miserable lives knowing how they took away our light, our love, and feel the emptiness that I feel for once, that I have felt for over forty years now.

I want them to know there is no closure. There is no salvation for the things they have done. God will not forgive them. I will not forgive them. All they can look forward to is burning. May they rot in hell for what they've done.

"You want to find an ending?" Jennings asks. "An ending life never gave you? Well, here's your chance."

I stare at him. The words are so simple, they shake me. "What're you saying?"

"Why not write the version of your story that real life can't? Give yourself the closure you're eager for. A real *wham bam thank you ma'am* finale. Go to town. Car chases, shoot-outs… the whole lot."

"But…" I start without knowing just what exactly I want to ask. "But what if that's not the way it—"

"You need to break out from that mindset," he cuts in. He shrugs. "You never know. It might be pretty liberating."

I want to be free. "I can do that? Really?"

"Go for it. Surprise yourself."

He clasps me on the shoulder and squeezes before stepping around me. He hadn't locked his door. I stand next to his car while he turns the engine over—once, twice, a few too many times, choking the valve before it finally heaved to life.

Give myself an ending. God, there's nothing I want more. Nothing in this world. I can finally give Billy the ending he deserves.

Closure.

ROUND AND ROUND

Her name is Leslie Givens.

At sixteen, she had tight curls of auburn hair that garlanded both ears. A pair of candy-apple cheeks round enough to pinch her eyes every time she smiled.

She looked as if she still had her baby teeth. Tiny white tombstones.

Before she married and became *Mrs. Reynolds*, six months shy of graduating from high school, Leslie had danced with my son.

The Dade County Fall Social always took place at the Paterson Rec Center the first weekend in November. The gymnasium was transformed into a corn-husk hideaway. The bleachers were pushed back, hidden behind hay bales and pumpkins. Orange and yellow crepe paper streamers were strung from the basketball net. The only athletic remnant was the center circle bull's-eyeing the polished floor. If you didn't look down, you'd never know this is where kids shot hoops after school.

The social began lord knows how many years back. Most likely when folks actually still farmed around here. The Shriners commandeered the shindig at some point to raise funds for themselves. A dollar a ticket to dance the night away.

Carol and I cut a rug there together when we were just kids first courting one another. The tone and tenor of the formal hasn't changed much since. Children come with their parents, adults and kids alike enjoying the apple cider and cookies.

Billy never was one for festivities, so it was a surprise when he asked us to go. "Is this a new leaf turning?" I couldn't help myself. I just had to rib him.

"Sure." His voice took a tone. "Can I go?"

Carol was more dubious than me. "What are you going to do?"

"What do you think?"

"Well, clearly you're not going to dance…"

"Who says I'm not?"

"Are you?"

"Maybe."

"Really? With who?"

"Friends."

"Which *friends*?"

"You want me to write out a list?"

"I want you to tell the truth."

Billy's head rolled over his shoulders. "Can I go or not?"

"Just let him go," I cut in, coming to Billy's rescue. "What's the harm?"

Carol gave me Look #32 for my troubles. So much for a unified front. "There's no harm if he actually does as he says," she intones, her voice quite steady for someone tamping down her annoyance. "I'm more worried he won't even go inside the rec center. I'm thinking he may end up hanging out in the parking lot all night."

"Come on, Mom… Please?"

"Be back by ten."

"Seriously?"

"You want to go or not?" Carol stared at me, daring me to defy her.

"But my curfew's eleven…"

"Your ass is back in this house by eleven," I said. "Not 11:10. Not even 11:01. You got me? Don't make me come down there and drag you home…"

"Got it."

Billy never mentioned Leslie in conversation. Her name never came up once. But it wasn't a surprise to learn he had a crush on her. Who wouldn't? If you were fortunate enough to be on the receiving end of her smile, you'd soften up, too.

Leslie had been going steady with another fellow who felt it was beneath him to dance in front of the rest of town. He'd rather get tipsy with his buddies in the parking lot, sneaking beers from the cover of his car when nobody was looking.

That left Leslie without a dance partner. She was free and clear to spend the evening with her girlfriends in the gym, sitting along the sidelines and gossiping.

The bargain basement sound system was sputtering out a steady stream of radio pop pap. Top 40 tunes wrapped everyone's conversation in a fuzzy blanket of feedback, drowning their voices out. If you wanted to be heard, you had to lean in and raise your voice.

Billy made his way up to Leslie. Walked right up to her. Simply stood there, awkwardly shifting side to side until the girls' conversation faded.

Leslie looked up and realized he was standing before her. An offering. A willing sacrifice for the dance floor.

"Wanna dance?" he asked, loud enough to be heard.

She understood what he'd said, but Leslie was coy enough to make him ask again anyway, leaning over and giving him her ear. "What was that?"

"I said…" Billy closed in. "Do. *You*. Wanna. *Dance?*"

Leslie's friends snorted back their giggles, giving Billy the quick up-down. They sized him up and found him lacking. *Who the heck is this punk, stepping out of the pecking order?* All pimples and ribs in a blue jean jacket.

But you know what? Leslie found it brave of Billy.

Standing there, like that. Before her. His demonstration of old-fashioned chivalry made her smile. It's the little things that make a difference. None of the other guys from school had dared come near these pretty young gals all night, pastel mermaids on display, as if the boys here were too afraid of the seniors outside, getting blotto in the parking lot.

Not my Billy. What did he have to lose? Tomorrow, this Brigadoon would revert back to its rigid athletic parameters. Nothing more than a basketball court once more, all free-throws and end-lines. But tonight, for another few hours, there was something magical in the air. A space like this only exists for one night out of the year, so for those young lovers not too afraid to show a little bit of courage in the face of adolescent apathy and open their hearts to each other, miracles can happen.

So, Leslie said yes.

Not out loud. She merely held out her hand for Billy to take like she was a princess receiving her suitor. She glanced over her shoulder at her sniggering girlfriends and stuck out her tongue, plucked from the sideline and drawn across the basketball court. Leslie knew they were just jealous, even if they'd never admit it.

Billy chose her.

She hooked her arm through his and let herself be escorted onto the dance floor, orange and yellow lights casting an amber haze across her exposed shoulders.

The DJ couldn't have timed the moment more perfectly. As these two stepped into the center circle, the song shifted to something much more languid. Romantic.

"Your Song" by Elton John eased out from the speakers as Leslie draped her arms over Billy's shoulders.

What Leslie didn't know, what she could never have prepared herself for, was that Billy really knew how to move. *This kid sure can dance,* she thought.

Billy had gotten his first taste of the dance floor at age eleven. His mother, bless her, had subjected him to cotillion as early as fifth grade. He loathed it at the time, kicking and screaming all the way. But it would come in handy one day. These formal balls had him promenading with suburban society girls, taking their dainty hands and stumbling through clumsy two-steps. Strutting the simple stuff. Waltzes, mainly. Fox trots. The East Coast Swing. Billy was well-versed in them all.

Proper dance parameters had always been pretty stringent back then. Girls' wrists were suspended over boys' shoulders, elbows locked for maximum detachment. Boys' hands were planted within the midrange of that vast expanse of torso, holding without *actually* gripping the midriff, touching without exploring the contours of that forbidden feminine terrain right there in the palms of our hands.

Hence the stiffened legs. The Frankenstein waltz.

The mannequin-like weight-shift in their feet: *Back-and-forth, back-and-forth, back-and-forth…*

But Elton John was getting under their skin. The song was working its spell over them. Nothing existed outside of his voice. The words. Nothing beyond this moment mattered. It was just the two of them, out there, suspended in amber.

I hope you don't mind…

Billy's fingers nestled within the delicate channels of his dance partner's ribcage. Every inhale caused her chest to swell, as if her ribs were gripping his hands from the other side of her dress. Her heartbeat radiated into him.

I hope you don't mind…

Billy takes her in. Sees her. When she looks back, seeing him, Billy leans in.

For a kiss.

Leslie lets him. The two close their eyes—and for a brief, bewitching moment, the song sends them off to some distant spot. No chaperones, no giggling children, no dancing classmates. It's just the two of them out there.

The song ends and the two separate. Leslie looks at Billy and immediately realizes it's best that they pull apart. *Now.* Before somebody sees them together.

They're not alone.

They never were.

When Alan Reynolds spotted Billy Partridge on the dance floor with his girlfriend, he gets it in his head that he's got to teach this kid a lesson. It doesn't help that he's drunk. There's a whirlpool of PBR whipping his head into a frenzy.

It definitely doesn't help that his friends are watching along with him.

Johnny Mannefort.

Walt Thompson.

His pals keep egging him on—*Watcha gonna do huh you can't let that punk get away with that if that was my girlfriend holy shit I would mess that bastard up…*

The florescent lights flicker to life overhead, blanching out everyone.

The magic dissipates.

Time to go home.

Billy's curfew is closing in on him. It'll be eleven before long. He's hoping to hitch a ride home.

The road leading out from the rec center is lined with parked cars. Billy's hoofing it back. He turns every so often to see if he can't flag down a passing car. So far, no luck. Nobody's stopping. It might be the jean jacket. *Who'd ever stop for him?*

That's when Walt Thompson pulls up in his Chevelle. The low rumble of the engine is a dead giveaway. He leans over and opens the passenger-side door.

"Hop on in," he says. Even pats the upholstery of the passenger side seat with the palm of his hand.

It's not a question. Not a *request*. The command is subtle, but it's there, embedded in the words.

Hop on in.

Billy spots Johnny and Alan in the backseat, still drinking. The smell of beer must've been on their breath, in everything. Yeast permeates the upholstery.

What choice does Billy have? Besides, the clock is ticking. Curfew is closing in. He knows who these guys are. Around here, who doesn't? Did Alan see him dancing with Leslie? Maybe he didn't. Maybe this is just a coincidence. Crazier things have happened. Alan doesn't look pissed. He's actually grinning from the backseat.

So, Billy climbs in. Sits shotgun.

Walt's gunning the gas before Billy can shut the door. He peels away with a holler, the wind picking up all around.

The speedometer climbs. Fifty… sixty… sixty-five miles per hour. The rec center is in the rearview mirror, shrinking by the second, until it disappears.

They drive in silence for a while. The radio is on, blasting out the windows. The music bounces off the woods, reverberating through the surrounding trees.

Seventy… eighty… eighty-five miles an hour.

Billy notices they've missed the turn for his house. He wants to ask where they're going—*Where are you taking me?*—but who could hear him?

Who'd listen?

Alan already has the duct tape out in the backseat. He peels off a strip right behind Billy's head. That high-pitched rip tears through the air, even with the music blaring. It's so close, the sound of peeling adhesive sends a vibration through the back of Billy's neck. That release of tape delivers a brittle shiver down his spine.

Johnny yanks back on Billy's seatbelt, pinning him in place while Alan wraps the tape around his mouth.

Then his nose.

His eyes.

Round and round it goes…

Walt pulls into the vacant lot. Whether the plan was to come here all along or if this was all improvised, it's anyone's guess—but here it is: A flat field. A forgotten gravel bed. Weeds rise from the rocks. Whatever building was destined to be built here has long been abandoned, leaving the remnants of construction to languish. A heap of sand soaked through. The outer plane of a foundation dug into the ground.

It will be decades before a developer picks up the property and puts together a strip mall—but tonight, this forgotten plot will be Billy's final resting place.

A 5.65-acre graveyard, all for him.

Walt tugs Billy out from the car by his legs, then drags him across the lot. Once they've gotten far enough from the car, he squats on top of his chest.

Johnny gets a kick in.

Then another.

Alan's watching on. Fuming from the sidelines. When Walt notices he's not participating, he insists he play. *Come on, man. Don't be such a pussy. Do it.*

So, Alan steps up. He reels his foot back and drives

it right into Billy's side. Billy twists his torso, writhing like a worm over the ground.

The second kick comes a lot faster. Alan realizes he has plenty of more kicks where that came from. So many more. He punts. And punts. And punts.

Billy's struggling under Walt, worming over the ground, but it's no good. The duct tape bubbles, his breath trapped in a capsule around his mouth. He's shouting. *Screaming.* But the sound is all wrong. It's muffled, muted. There's nothing to hear. Nobody to help. He's all alone out here.

Something jabs Walt in his hip. He reaches into his pocket and discovers he snatched a permanent marker from work without realizing it. He just got a job at the box factory, working part-time alongside his pops and everybody else in this town.

An epiphany hits.

Struck with a moment of drunken inspiration, Walt pulls the top off the permanent marker with his teeth and—still sitting on Billy, pinning him in place as the boy suffocates—he sketches a pair of crude circles for eyes. They warp and wobble but now Billy can stare blankly back at them as Alan gets in another kick.

They're all laughing now. He looks pretty funny, doesn't he?

Those eyes. *What a gas!* Talk about a real riot. *Look at him!*

Those eyes don't blink. *Whatcha looking at, Billy, huh?* Just staring at nothing.

Got something to say, Billy? What's that? I can't hear you…

Speak up! Speak up, Billy!

By the time Walt realizes Billy isn't struggling anymore, he stands.

They're all waiting for Billy to breathe.

To budge.

To blink.

But those eyes, those wobbly circles, they only stare blankly back.

KILL YOUR DARLING

I t takes a moment to realize what I've done. The empty pages at the back of the scrapbook are littered with scribbles, cellophane skin peeled away and tattooed.

I barely recognize my own handwriting. The letters are loose, unraveled. I don't even remember writing them.

What have I done? What have I done?

My boy. My baby boy.

My wrist is sore. The arthritis seethes through my fingers. I can't keep my hand from trembling when I finally write—

The end

—and gently close the scrapbook, as if I'm tucking Billy into bed.

FRESH EYES

Another coughing fit drags me out of my sleep. The phlegm has thickened itself in my chest so much, it feels like cement sealing over a well.

I couldn't have been asleep for long. My wrist is still cramping from writing. How I even dragged myself into bed is beyond me. Must've shuffled upstairs and promptly passed out, short-lived as it is.

I find myself in bed. Alone. Have to get my bearings.

Where's Carol?

The guest room. Of course. Lost myself for a moment, there. Completely slipped my mind that she's still sleeping downstairs.

I crawl out of bed. Head for the restroom. This cough is only getting worse.

A glass of water brings me to the kitchen. My throat's so dry, I take down two glasses before heading back upstairs. I won't be able to get back to sleep at this point, but so it goes. Another night shuffling through the shadows of our house.

There's a stillness to the living room. It's a goddamn wonder I don't knock into more furniture, but I've grown so accustomed to the pathways through our house, tightening my flight patterns, I could wander around with my eyes closed.

I hear breathing.

A sibilant hiss. Sounds like squeezing the air out through a hole in a balloon, thin and faint and high-pitched, but it's there. In the dark. An asthmatic rasp.

Someone's sitting on the couch.

I don't say anything, letting my eyes settle. Their head looks like an egg.

They're not moving.

Just breathing.

Wheezing.

My eyes adjust to the dark, taking in the shadows. I see their head is wrapped in duct tape. The mottled contours of the mask pulse with every labored breath, bulging at odd spots along their face, trapped air hissing out through the fissures.

I see the eyes. The wobbling permanent marker.

A gray boy.

"Billy?"

He turns his head at the sound of his name, duct tape crinkling along his neck. Wisps of cornsilk hair poke out from the adhesive creases, like weeds reaching out from cracks in drab concrete. Those warped eyes never blink, staring at me.

Billy's breathing picks up. The strips of tape bubble and hiss all around his head. The air wants out, to escape, but there's not enough space in the tape for his exhales to slip through, spitting out of each and every last crevasse around his head.

He's suffocating all over again.

I reach for the lamp on the night stand table, just next to the couch.

"Billy—"

The second I turn the lamp on, filling the room with light—

The gray boy is gone.

It's Carol. She's sitting right where Billy just was. The scrapbook is open in her lap. The album is held up by the armrests of her wheelchair.

She's been reading my book. *The Book of Billy.*

"What have you done?" she asks before she even looks up from its pages. I can see she's been crying. It's hard to read the expression on her face. She seems confused. *Hurt.* But now that she's staring at me, eyes tightening, she looks horrified.

"What is this?" Her voice is brittle. The question comes out of her throat in a croak.

"That's him," I say. "That's Billy."

"This," she stabs the open page with her finger, until the scrapbook collapses from its perch upon the armrests and into her lap. "This is not our son."

"It's how I want to remember him."

"But this isn't how it happened!"

"How can we know?"

This takes Carol back, I can tell. She shakes her head, lips parted. She wants to say something. "You're making things up… because it makes you feel *better*?"

"That book keeps him alive!"

Our voices are raising now. It disturbs the air. The miasma that has hung throughout this house stirs. The fine yellow feathering of Post-Its clinging to the walls bristle the louder we shout.

"Is this because of the workshop? Are you still mad at me for signing you up?" Her eyes widen. Something has just occurred to her. "Have you *shared* this?"

"It's his story." I say it so calmly, so evenly, it sends a chill through the room.

"You're giving him away," she says. "You're letting him go."

"No…" I step forward. Carol reels back, sinking deeper into her wheelchair. Retreating from me, as if I'd raised a fist. She doesn't recognize me at all.

I kneel before her wheelchair, straining on my way down.

I take the scrapbook away. Close it up. Once I place it on the ground, out of Carol's sight, I reach back for her hands. They're clasped together in her lap, much smaller than I remember. Blue veins lace the knot of her hands, a poorly giftwrapped present I'll never open, so I simply place my hands on top of hers.

"He'll always be here. With us."

I'm lower than her now, so she has to look down at me. Dazed. It's unclear if she believes me or not. But she unwraps her hands and folds mine into hers.

I bow my head into her lap, kissing the tangle of our fists, while she presses her lips against the back of my skull.

"How could you?" she asks.

That's the last time Carol will ever pester me to read my book.

OPEN MIC

The librarians have pulled out their folding chairs from storage. Three even rows in the children's section. The shelving units are on wheels, so all the librarians have to do is simply push them back against the wall and the space opens up.

The books are still here, surrounding me. Picture-board books with mottled corners. Fairy tales and dog-eared fantasy novels. *Where the Sidewalk Ends. A Wrinkle in Time.* Their covers have faded over the years. Spines gnawed on. Most kids choose to chew through these books rather than read them.

This is wrong. It feels inappropriate to bring Billy out amongst all these innocent stories. Fairies and knights and dinosaurs. What I'm about to do is practically sacrilege. *I can't do this. Please don't make me do this.*

I remember Carol and Billy tucking themselves

off into a corner back here and reading their Saturday afternoons away. Billy would curl into Carol's lap, a book open before them. She'd lean her chin over his shoulder and read right into his ear, whispering these stories. This was their space. This is where her memories live.

And here I am, about to piss all over it.

This is it. The Big Night. *Christ.* Jennings warned us from day number one that this moment was coming, *hell or high water*, but I didn't think he'd actually make us.

Shouldn't this sort of thing be optional? Why is it mandatory? I shouldn't have to do this. Not in front of people. Not in front of our town.

Christ, not in front of Carol.

I catch a glance of her through the bookshelves as she's wheeled into the front row. The librarian takes away one of the folding chairs to make room for her. She's got ringside seats now, wearing this anxious look on her face that I haven't seen in a long time. She's worried. About me. She thinks I'm going to make a fool out of myself. She's probably right. Wouldn't be the first time.

Carol will never forgive me for this.

Talk about a small crowd. Friends and family. Can't imagine they're here for the catering. There's a spread of stale Entenmann's and watered-down coffee. A tower of Styrofoam cups just next to the sugar packs and creamer. At least at AA, the conversation was a little more lively. This feels downright funereal.

I pass the time before the festivities kick off by playing a little guessing game. *Who's-here-for-who.* Try matching folks in the crowd with the writers from class.

Siobhan's husband is easy pickings. The suit. The wan expression easing down his face. Sweating like he's in the hot seat. He's checked his watch three times.

Gonna be a long night, pal...

For all of us.

Jennings makes his way out in front of the crowd. There's a smattering of polite applause. Nobody's quite sure how to handle themselves here. What to expect.

They're not alone.

"Thank you for making it out tonight." Jennings gives his spiel, laying it on thick. "Are you in for a treat. I couldn't be prouder. These writers have all put in a lot of hard work these last few weeks. Donna Tartt's got nothing on these guys!"

He smirks at his own joke, but the audience barely musters a smile. *Who the heck is Donna Tartt? Does she live up the street?*

"I must say..." Jennings clears his throat. "When we first started this workshop, I didn't know what to expect. Writing is about discipline. It's about craft."

I spot Carol squirming in her chair.

"That's not something you're born with. That takes hard work. Patience. I'm pleased to say, the pieces you are about to hear tonight are the fruit of the discipline and determination of some very talented first-time authors. Let's hear their stories!"

Sarah reads first. That gal's been itching to share her story about romancing some half-man, half-cat ever since she brought her pages in to class. The passages focusing on flesh caressing fur seem to go on a hair bit too long for most of the audience's comfort, but she's relishing this. Folks kindly golf clap once she finishes.

Siobhan reads next. I'm having fun watching her husband squirm. His neck reddens around the collar. He's choking under his tie.

One of the high school girls doesn't even show. The other reads for less than a few minutes. I'm having a hard time concentrating. My mind's elsewhere.

I can't do this. I can't do this. I can't—

Before we began, Jennings found me in the back. "Anxious?"

I grunted.

"Don't worry. They say if you get a bad case of stage-fright, the best thing to do is imagine your audience naked."

"Who's *they*?"

"It's just something people say. Try it. See if it helps."

Something about seeing Carol slumped over in her wheelchair without any clothes on doesn't sit right. She's in the bathtub. Her sunken chest droops over the knobs of her knees. Those thin toothpick arms. Seeing her naked like this brings out her eyes. Makes them look bigger. I've done this to her. Exposed her. This is all my fault. Dragging her through this. She'll never forgive me. She probably never should.

"Our last story for the night is one of the more pleasant surprises from the group," Jennings says during my introduction. "I didn't know what to expect from Glenn when he first came into class. He kept his cards pretty close to his chest throughout the workshop. It was a tug-of-war to get him to share." He hesitates, reflecting on something that seems to bring him happiness. "I'm happy he did."

Brooke Jennings turns and offers me a smile. There's something disarming about it, the warmth of it. I don't know what he's thinking, but he looks gratified.

Proud. He looks genuinely honored.

"Everybody, please give a hand to our final reader. Glenn Partridge…"

The applause sounds soft. All I hear is skin smacking skin. Faint backhands all around, chasing after me as I step up in front of the crowd.

I'm having a hard time breathing. I cough, bringing up something solid from my chest. I've got nowhere to spit, so I swallow it back down.

I can't focus. The words keep squirming across the page. Writhing, like a body over the dry ground of a vacant lot. I bring the paper up to my face and pinch my eyes for a moment, just to get my focus back, but the words won't stay still.

Maggots. Every letter.

The words twist and turn in front of me, worming their way over the page like they're boiling out from the carcass of some dead animal. I'm not seeing paragraphs and sentences anymore, but the pecked-over skeleton of a fawn. They've devoured this baby deer down to the bone. There won't be anything left of my story.

I'm not strong enough to do this. I thought I could, but I can't.

I'm not strong enough.

I'm not brave.

Carol's looking at me. She's just as terrified as I am—either for me or for what I'm about to do. The silence that spreads through the crowd only thickens. The seconds extend themselves, stretching out. Coagulating. The air is so thick in here.

This story is a recitation. A spell to invoke the dead. These words will bring him back, but at a price. An incantation as strong as this can kill the conjurer.

Maybe it should.

I can feel the sweat pebbling on my forehead. My lungs feel like grain sacks filled to their hilt. The air just won't go in. Somebody is sitting on me. Squatting on my chest. Pinning me in place. I can't get up. Can't move. Can't breathe. I cough once more, then again. The gray phlegm is clogging up my throat.

I'm going to choke, drown in front of all these people, on my own two feet.

I'm going to drown.

I can't do this.

I can't…

I hear the tape peeling just behind my ear. It's weaving around my head. I close my eyes just as it winds around and I settle into that darkness. The tape keeps turning, peeling off the roll, the shrill rip of it circling my head once, twice, three times. It continues to wrap itself around me, muffling all sound, all light, all air.

The library fades away. It's so dark in here. There's no light anymore.

I can't do this. I can't breathe. Can't—

Billy slowly comes into focus. He's six. Sitting Indian-style right in front of me, wearing his Spider-Man PJs. Webs all up and down his legs.

I remember this memory.

Carol was visiting her family, leaving me and Billy at home for the weekend. We ordered pizza for three dinners in a row. Ate ice cream for lunch. Watched the midnight creature feature, even though we both knew he'd have nightmares.

Now it was time for bed. "Tell me a story," he insists. Actually demanded it. For such a little sprite, he sure could be a pint-sized tyrant when he wanted to be.

"I don't think I've got a story," I said. "That's your mom's department."

"Just tell me one. *Please?*"

"Want me to read you a book or something? I can't get one…"

"No. I want a story."

"What kind of story?" I'm at a loss here. I'm really terrible at this.

"Anything. Just tell it."

I think about it for a while and then I tell him a story about a boy who danced with a beautiful girl and paid an unfathomable price for it. It wasn't his fault. None of it was this kid's fault. The world was just too cruel for him. But so it goes in stories.

The story comes out so easily. Flows from me. Everything else melts away after those first few sentences. It's just me and the tale being told and it rings true.

PRODUCT PLACEMENT

*D*ear Relieve…

Flip to page four of this morning's paper and you'll find a photo of my son.

Hadn't planned on finding him there, to be honest. Didn't expect to open up the early edition today and see him lying in the lot all over again. But there he is—sprawled out along the gravel lot, just how the police found him forty years ago.

Only now he's book-ended between ads for ladies' lingerie and pain relievers.

Instead of paramedics and police officers, Billy is surrounded by women in their bras and panties. The ditch is lined with clearance sales, as if his body had been dumped into some department store instead. All these price-tags bristle in the wind, as fragile as the thickets growing along the road. Marked-down prices, slashed in half.

I've never seen this photo before. It must have been taken after the police found him. How the newspaper got their hands on it is beyond me.

Most people probably wouldn't even recognize Billy from the way he's facing the camera. The duct tape covering his head keeps his features hidden. Luckily, the photo is from the back. The picture doesn't show the front of his face. But if you squint, if you strain your eyes hard enough, taking in every pixel, all those tiny dots of newsprint form into his body. His hand slung out at his side. Suddenly... it's Billy.

Your ad is printed directly next to his left shoulder.

Nine out of ten doctors recommend Relieve *more than any other brand of pain reliever sold in supermarkets today. For the temporary reprieve of headaches, backaches, and all the other aches and pains your body can muster—choose relief. Choose* Relieve!

There's this woman holding up a bottle to the camera. Smiling. Acting as if your product is the answer to all her prayers. You can tell she's not hurting anymore.

She's sitting next to Billy, like they're friends posing for the same picture. There's barely any border between the two photographs, the line dividing your ad from his picture blurring together.

It's funny how, if you take two completely opposing photos and place them right next to each other—suddenly, without thinking about it, your eye will unconsciously connect them together. Your mind automatically turns them into one.

Here I am, sitting in the kitchen this morning. The newspaper's open. And here's this article about my son's murder. The headline practically slaps me in the face:

One Man's Perseverance Paves the Way for a New Ending.

Only I can't read it. I can't take in the words. All I can do is look at the ads surrounding Billy. I'm sticking with the pictures, until I'm linking lingerie with suffocating duct tape, asphyxiation with child-proof bottle caps.

And here's this complete stranger, some model I've never met before kneeling next to my son, telling me how I can stop hurting. Who in the hell is this gal?

The intimacy of the images has turned them into some sort of morbid compare and contrast with one another:

This is what you feel like before you take Relieve—and this is after.

My boy has become some spokesperson for your product. You've incorporated his death into your ad campaign. You're endorsing his murder. He's modeling for you, for Christ's sake. His face was pummeled to a pulp—but pop two caplets every couple hours and the pain will just melt away, am I right?

"Up to eight hours of relief?"

"Satisfaction guaranteed?"

You know what pain relievers really are? They're chemical barricades. Road-blocks between your brain and nerve-endings.

Why am I telling you this stuff? Of course you know this. It's your product, for Christ's sake. You made the damn thing. But maybe it's time for a reminder: Every time you stub your toe, studies show your body releases these chemicals that transmit pain signals through your nervous system, informing the rest of yourself that you have to <u>hurt</u> now. Now it's time to <u>ache</u>. But pop some ibuprofen and those injured cells can't release that chemical anymore. It stops your body from sending the message.

It doesn't heal you. Doesn't cure you. It just keeps you from feeling anything.

Toothaches. Muscle aches. Every ache and pain your body can muster just…

Washes away.

So how about heartache? How many caplets would I have to swallow to stop myself from feeling the way I do now? How many bottles would I have to buy?

Wasn't until I opened this morning's newspaper that I got to see him again. I promised my wife I wouldn't go back to the lot. It's been at least a decade since I set foot out there. Maybe more. They built this strip mall over it twenty years ago. Filled it with pizzerias and 99 cent shops full of junk. We never shopped there. This was the monument to my son. A shopping plaza nobody needed, full of stores nobody wanted.

Before they built it, for years, I'd drop off a bouquet directly on the spot where they found Billy's body. I know he's buried in some cemetery, but this was where I wanted to remember my son. This spot, this little patch of unpaved ground, where he was last alive, where he breathed his last—this was his final resting place for me.

Now it's a parking lot.

The mall shuttered down. One business after another went under, closing up. The plaza just sits there, all empty. Weeds reach up from the cracks in the asphalt.

But with the picture they printed in this morning's newspaper, it's as if I'm there. It's that night all over again. Only now, nobody's telling me to stand back. I can walk through the lot. Go wherever I want to go. No cop is going to stop me.

Seeing Billy on the ground, surrounded by all those women parading around in their half-priced panties — it looks like Billy is nothing more than some awkward model, posing with the rest of them. He must've tripped just as the shutter snapped.

I'm pushing through the crowd, forcing my way past all the models in their underwear, running right up to Billy. He is pixilated now. His body is all grainy to me. I can't see him so well. I know I'm not supposed to, but I start peeling away the duct tape. I'm tearing through the shell encased around his head. He might still be breathing under there. I have to try.

I finally reach his face. His skin is all smudged from a misprint. The color tones are off by an inch, shifting tints from their proper spot. The color of his eyes is now on his cheek, the green deviating from his irises, leaving the sockets all empty. There's newspaper ink smeared all over my fingers, his blood, but the red has bled elsewhere.

Billy? *I call out.* Billy, can you hear me?

I want to hold him. I want to pick him up and take him back home. I want to comb the hair out of his face and carry him back to our house. I want to brush the color of his eyes back into the right place, sweeping the green off his cheeks.

Billy, it's me. It's your dad. I'm right here, son. I'm with you now.

I look over to my side and I notice the woman kneeling next to us. She's looking right at me. Smiling. Not a care in the world. She doesn't feel a goddamn thing. She holds this bottle up to me, the caplets rattling inside, and says—Use only as directed.

I walked away from the newspaper and went straight to our medicine chest, sifting through the shaving cream and toothpaste until I found them. Waiting for me.

Each container of Relieve holds a hundred caplets. Each caplet holds six hundred milligrams of that magic ingredient acetaminophen. Not to mention corn starch. Hydroxyethyl cellulose. Hydroxypropyl methylcellulose. Magnesium stearate. Microcrystalline cellulose. Povidone. Powdered cellulose. Pregelatinized starch. Sodium starch glycolate. Titanium dioxide. Triacetin.

So tell me. I want to know: Which ingredient will relieve me?

I went ahead and popped the child-proof cap with my thumb and brought the bottle right up to my lips. Just tilted my neck back and began chewing. This rusty tasting paste overwhelmed my mouth, but I swallowed it all down.

You should put me in one of your ads. Let me be a testament to pain relief.

Let's see how many bottles I sell for you.

Signed—

ART IMITATING LIFE

I t wasn't a suicide attempt. For the love of Christ, I'm nearly eighty now. Why in the hell would I kill myself now? I've made it this far. What would be the point?

I know how it must've looked. I'm not saying Carol shouldn't have reacted the way she did, but calling an ambulance and dragging my discombobulated ass to the hospital just to get my stomach pumped is not how I wanted to spend my Saturday.

This was all a big misunderstanding. I wasn't trying to kill myself, I swear.

I had to convince the doctor I wasn't a suicide risk. He wouldn't release me unless he was a hundred percent positive. All the nurses were looking at me like I was some sad-sack suicidal senior citizen they all got to shine a little sun upon.

There's so much to live for, sugar...

They probably read the article.

Jesus, they all know. I'm a celebrity now. A circus freak making up stories about his dead son. Everybody looks at me like I got a screw loose. Pitying me.

Carol hasn't talked to me since we got home. She thinks I was clocking out on her. Abandoning her in this house. "It's not what you think," I say. "Hand to God."

"What was it then?"

"An accident."

"Downing a whole bottle of painkillers? That's an accident?"

"It was stupid of me, I know… But I wasn't leaving you. I'll never leave you."

Carol's staring me down. Sussing me up like she doesn't know who the hell I am. Who is this stranger that's taking the place of her husband?

"Why didn't you tell me?"

"Tell you what?"

"I spoke with your doctor…"

"About?"

"What do you think?"

"Beats the hell out of me…"

"You lied to me," she says.

Wasn't expecting that curve-ball. She must've spoke to the doctor when I was under. *Goddamn it.* Cat's out of the bag now, I guess. No point denying it.

"I didn't want you to worry."

Carol smacks me. Her palm plants itself straight across my cheek. It's a weak hit, but the sentiment behind it is what really stings. "The doctor said you knew. That there was time to treat it, but you never scheduled *the goddamn appointment*."

She's spitting out the words, getting me wet.

What can I tell her?

What can I say?

It's true. I knew—and I decided to live with him. I want to tell her it was my choice. I want to keep him inside me. But she wouldn't understand. Nobody would.

It's Billy. Don't you see? He's here. Inside me.

I needed to lay down. Rest for a spell. There's a burning sensation running the length of my trachea from where they ran the tube down my throat.

My head's killing me. I thought the whole point to Relieve is they take your headache away—but I've got a worse migraine now than ever before. This dull thud throbs through my skull. My pulse is pummeling my ear drums, slowly and steady. It lifts in pitch. Sharpens itself. Now it's picking up the pace, ringing louder. Louder.

The phone. The phone is ringing next to my bed. It won't stop chiming.

How long has it been ringing?

What time is it? The sun isn't even up yet. It's dark outside.

I just closed my eyes for a minute…

Coughing. Always coughing. My windpipe clogged with phlegm. I have to hack it up and spit it out, just to keep breathing.

"Hello?" I don't even recognize the sound of my own voice.

"Mr. Partridge?"

"Yes?"

"Did I wake you?" A woman's voice. Detective Corrigan. When was the last time we'd talked? How long has it been since she reached out to me? Usually, I had to hunt her down just to get her to return a call. This—this was something else.

Something's wrong.

"No—I'm awake." There's no hiding the anxiousness in my voice. "Did you find something? Is there anything new?"

Anything new.

There's nothing new under the sun, my workshop instructor's voice seeps into my head. *No new stories. Only new ways of telling them.*

So what's your story, Glenn?

Maybe she heard about the hospital visit. Jesus, is she just checking in on me? Make sure that I'm not going to hang myself? I'm never going to live this one down.

"I wanted to call," she hesitates. There's an added texture to her voice. Something I haven't heard in her before. Guilt, maybe? Remorse? Corrigan's never been easy to read. "I wanted to call so that you heard it from me first."

I sit upright and immediately regret it. My chest clamps, as if my ribs tighten their grip around my lungs. I clutch at my breast, massaging the muscles there.

"Did you find something?"

Silence from the other end. She's deciding how best to say this. Whatever this is. "There's been—there's been a wrinkle in the case. It could complicate matters."

What is she getting at?

Was it the article? It has to be. That goddamn article. She's going to scold me for crossing the line. *Meddling.* Making her job more difficult by making up stories.

Treating me like a child.

"Listen," I jump right in, ready to give her a piece of my mind. "I didn't think anyone would ever read it. Had I known the newspaper was going to be—"

"Mr. Partridge."

"What's done is done. We've all got to live with it. Me more than anyone else."

"Mr. Partridge, please—"

"But I've been wait—"

"Alan Reynolds shot himself."

The phone nearly slips through my fingers. I can feel it slide down my palm, slick with fresh sweat. I have to tighten my grip before it drops to the floor.

"I shouldn't be calling, but… I knew you'd want to know."

"Killed himself?"

"At home." Corrigan edits out key details. She

doesn't have to tell me. Thanks to the creative writing workshop, I'm able to envision what happened all by myself.

Here. Let me paint a picture for you: Some cub reporter from the local Courier came to cover our workshop's reading at the local library. Just a simple wrap-up of the event, frivolous from start to finish. A puff piece. Nothing more.

Then I haul my ass up to read—and suddenly, my story hijacks the whole evening. I became the story. Or, more to the point—my story was now the story.

Talk about an angle—*Some old coot takes it upon himself to play amateur Dashiell Hammett for a spell, spin some yarn about his kid getting killed many a moon ago. He never got justice, so he kicks up some cobwebs to see if he can't get the ending his kid never got. This old man tells the story the way he wants to and gives this cold case the ending fate never had in the cards. And who's gonna stop him? Who could?*

But this old coot names names. Implicates members of the community. Very publicly. What's only been whispered at up to this point—it's now out in the open.

What doe-eyed, wet-behind-the-ears journo-jockey could pass up a story like that? Beats a puff piece like "Local Writers Share New Works," hands down.

Pulitzer, here we come…

The article makes its way into the paper. Like anybody's going to read it, I figured. This will all blow over. At best, I'd have to pretend to be a local celebrity the next time Carol and I went to the market—*Read the article, Glenn! Fair play to you!*

Who subscribes to the newspaper these days anyway? Certainly not Walt Thompson. Not Alan Reynolds or Johnny Mannefort.

But an old high school girlfriend of a cousin of Leslie Reynolds sure does. She gives her old gal pal a call and chews her ear off for a few, gabbing about the article—*Isn't that the kid your cousin was dancing with? The night of the fall dance?*

As soon as the two hang up, this cousin gives Leslie a ring and pretty much launches right into it, grilling her kin for the next hour.

This is how it works around these parts. In a town this small, no goddamn deed goes unpunished. People will find out, one way or another.

Leslie doesn't waste much time before speed-dialing her husband; he's still at the bar with his friends. She lays into him pretty thick, hissing into his ear— *He's been talking about you! He's writing about it!!* He hangs up and sits with the news, wondering what's the best course of action here. He orders another round.

Then another.

Before long, Alan Reynolds souses himself up with enough Johnny Walker Red to shuffle home and swallow the spitting end of his .38. Empties a round down the back of his throat in front of his wife of thirty-eight years. Paints the faux wood paneling of his trailer with brain matter. Bits of his skull still cling to the stucco.

"Still there, Mr. Partridge?"

Detective Corrigan has been considerate enough to let the news settle in for a spell, but the silence has gone on long enough now. She's ready to bring me back.

"Yeah." I cough. A little too wet. I swallow the phlegm back. "Yes. Still here."

"This is some pretty sensitive information. You understand that, yes? You must take all this with an enormous grain of salt."

"Yes." Then, a stilted breath later. "I understand."

"This is not public knowledge. Not yet."

Word travels like a wildfire. I hope it burns this whole goddamn town right to the ground.

"Thank you," I say.

"I needed you to hear it from me. Not from some beauty parlor gossip. But you need to be careful with this. I don't want you to get your hopes up."

Too late.

My heart. I feel my heart swelling in my chest. It's blooming. The years are flaking away.

"Don't jump to any conclusions, okay? This in of itself isn't damnable in any way. It could mean something. Or nothing. I'm thinking it means nothing."

It means I was right. It means I was onto something. The right track.

The truth.

That son of a bitch has been sitting on this, tamping his guilt down for forty years—and here I come along, some fucking old fart with a yarn, blabbing my mouth off to a bunch of librarians. That's all it took. There's the tipping point. After all these years. But instead of coming clean, Alan Reynolds chokes down his Remington and fires off one hell of an exclamation point at the end of his conscience.

Means nothing. It's fucking *everything*.

It means Alan Reynolds did this to my son.

Alan Reynolds killed my boy.

Alan—

"—Reynolds has had a fairly thorough history of alcoholism," Detective Corrigan continues. "Domestic battery. We're thinking he just decided to punch his clock and call it a day." Or the guilt got to him. Ate him up like cancer. A gray ghost haunting him from the inside. *Good riddance.* I nearly say it out loud, but think twice.

"I'm aware you and Mr. Reynolds have had some *conflicts*. You've been very vocal with your opinions about him. You know there are people in town who won't take kindly to your… recent activities."

"What about it?" I ask. Enough of this.

"Just—please, Mr. Partridge. Be careful, okay? Don't do anything that might agitate the situation. Let us look into all of this. I promise I'll get back to you as soon as I know something." When I don't respond, she asks, "Promise me, Mr. Partridge?"

"Yeah. Yeah, sure. Whatever you say."

"And if anyone approaches you, *anybody*, I want you to call me, okay? Doesn't matter what time of day or night it is. I'm going to give you my cell number…"

She won't come out and say it, but I know what she's getting at.

She's warning me about what I've written.

Everybody's a critic.

FAN MAIL

The brick shatters our kitchen window.

Carol had been setting the table. Only two places tonight. She's done pretending. We're left with just ourselves now.

I had been in the living room, flipping through the photo album, when I heard a brittle burst in the air. It sounded as if Carol dropped a plate. Several plates. A shower of ceramics. I rushed into the kitchen and found the floor covered in glass.

Out the window, I hear an engine accelerate. Red brake lights flash before slipping away. I can't tell for sure, but I swear I see Marina Blue. Convertible top.

Carol shrinks in her wheelchair. Her chest lifts and collapses with every breath, hefting the rest of her frame with it, her body a leather billows fanning a fire.

"Are you okay?" I ask, running to her.

Carol's eyes remain focused on the floor. On the

crimson intruder resting just a few inches away from her feet.

"Are you hurt?"

Carol shakes her head.

I check her lap for glass. None. "Are you sure you're okay?"

Carol nods.

It's a brick. Just a regular brick. Red clay. It could've come from anywhere, picked up from any countless amounts of construction sites around town.

But it's found its way through our window. Into our house.

Our home.

It's wrapped in newspaper. The local Courier. I pick it up, feel the brick's weight in my hand, the strain in my arm.

Peeling away the newspaper, I notice the headline. The photo. Billy's pixilated body resting in the lot, the grayscale blurring his hood of duct tape.

Whoever did this took a Sharpie marker and drew a new pair of black circles across the photo, directly over Billy's face.

Fresh eyes.

RESEARCH TRIP

The Chevelle rests on cinderblocks in the front yard. Its tires are gone, replaced by a quartet of concrete pedestals. Rust gnaws at its underbelly.

A blue tarp drapes over the front hood. A quick lift and I see the hood is missing. No engine inside anymore. Just the gutted chassis, all hollow.

It rests there on the front lawn like a forgotten totem. A reminder of past glories. Even I can remember its engine tearing through the neighborhood at night, all those years ago. Striking some sense of domestic terror in us all.

Now it's just a rusted relic. The bones of some abandoned prehistoric behemoth left to rot off into the ground.

Rust to rust...

I peer through the passenger-side window. Tufts of upholstery spill out from the torn seat.

I have a flash of Billy sitting there. The night plays out before me—I can see him staring out the windshield as the car picks up speed. Watch him wrestle against the boys in the back, pulling on his seatbelt until it cinched him in place.

The roll of duct tape comes out, Alan Reynolds peeling off a strip and sealing Billy's mouth. His eyes. It strikes me that this car—this windshield, whatever view passing through—this was the last thing Billy ever saw before it all went dark.

The house is a single-story family rancher in the midst of some hefty renovations. A bed of red bricks lay off to the side, covered in another blue tarp. It's been raining off and on these last few weeks, leaving whatever work that had to be done sealed up until sunnier weather prevails. The lawn itself is in sore need of a mow. Wet grass brushes up against my ankles. It's tallest around the Chevelle, a ring of weeds weaving through the cinderblocks and grabbing hold of the chassis.

"Can I help you?"

It doesn't take long to recognize the man standing on the front porch. I've seen him operating the forklift at the factory. His paunch has widened since I last saw him. Lost a bit more of his hair—but then again, who am I to judge?

Here it is, two in the afternoon, and Walt Thompson still hasn't gotten dressed. He's wearing a bathrobe and pajama bottoms. A white t-shirt that isn't so white anymore.

I don't say anything. Simply stare back. Let him stew for a spell.

Then it hits. I see it sink in. The pinch in his eyes slackens. His mouth opens.

Now he knows. Knows exactly who I am.

That's the look I'm hoping for.

I want him to be afraid.

The muscles in his face tighten. Whatever slack that unraveled his features seizes up again. He's not going to indulge me. He's not afraid. Not of some old coot.

"The fuck do you want?" Nothing but bile. He has to be in his late fifties. Maybe older by now. Whatever hair is left up top has gone gray, well on its way to white.

This is what's left of him. Nothing but a bitter man.

I hold up the brick. I haven't compared it to the ones in the stack, but I'd speculate that they are one of the same. It's so heavy in my hands. My shoulder muscles pinch. I can't hold it for much longer, but I present it to him.

"You dropped this."

I lob the brick into the air. Takes all the strength I have, but boy, is it glorious, watching that brick take flight. It hovers above his Chevelle for a brief, brilliant moment before gravity grips the brick and drops it directly onto the car's windshield, fracturing the smooth surface into a web of glass.

Walt lunges forward, ready to charge.

Then he halts.

I don't quite know what to expect from him. How he'll react. This is all uncharted territory, for both of us. I simply hold my ground.

Walt's jaw tightens. Grinds his teeth. His hands are fists just itching to find my face. "I'm within my rights to shoot. Don't think I won't."

Hearing him speak, after all these years—what can I say? I expect more from him. His voice sounds desperate. The bitterness doesn't appeal to me.

My silence works over on him. I can tell he doesn't like it.

"You want me to call the cops? Is that it, old man?"

Old man. It's so easy for us to fall into these clichéd characterizations. He should take a writing workshop. We assume these roles too quickly. He still acts like such a kid. A rotten child, even though there's nothing left, no youth, within him.

"By all means," I offer. "Give them a ring."

"You think I won't?" He's doubling down. He feels the threat, senses himself backing into the corner. What's left but to push back? "I got nothing to say to you. You best mind your own fucking business and get the fuck off my property."

I step forward.

Walt steps back. In that moment, the dynamic is on full display for both of us. He might not be afraid of me, but he sure as hell is afraid of what I stand for.

There's no pleasure in this. This isn't why I'm here. I can tell he's been fretting over this, this magic moment, for years now. Decades.

I don't want it. His fear gives me nothing. I'm too old for it. I hold out my hand, palm up, as if to offer my fingers for a stray dog to sniff, showing him that I mean no harm. "I want to see," I say.

Walt's face slackens.

"Show me." I take another step. "Show me what happened."

"The hell are you going on about?"

"I want to see. With my own eyes. Show me." I'm at the porch now, standing before him. I haven't dropped my hand, still holding it out, half-expecting him to bite. The weight of my arm causes my hand to quiver, but I keep it between us.

Walt remains on the stoop. The added height gives him an elevated perspective on me. He has to look down. "You serious?" He grins. In his mind, he's gotten a grip of the situation. Now he knows why I'm here, what I'm after—and he can't help but chuckle. "Jesus. This is—*shit*, man. Ain't this just fucking rich?"

I won't let up. I've come too far. No turning back now. "I want to see."

"Christ." He shakes his head. "You're not gonna let this go, are you? You're just gonna keep on keeping on until you keel over… "

"I want to see."

"*Stop saying that.*" His voice carries through the air.

There are other houses nearby. Neighbors would find this encounter far too tempting to look away from, were they to catch wind of it—so Walt quiets down. "There ain't nothing to see."

"Show me."

His fist raises. The anger is still there, still engrained into his body, his wasting muscles. A punch from him would sprawl me across the ground. But I'd get back up. I'd get back up and I'd hold my hand out to him again and again, so help me.

"I want to see."

"Shut up." There's something in his eye. An unraveling. They're getting wet. They look like oysters to me. All gray. His sockets look like they're full of phlegm.

"Please," I say. "I just want to—»

"Shut the fuck up!"

Does this man want absolution? Could I offer it to him? Is it within me to give him the release that he needs, after all these years? Could anybody give it to him?

"Please," I say. It comes out so quiet. Barely above a whisper. "*Please.*"

He's not even looking at me anymore. His mind is off elsewhere. At first, I don't think he heard me. Then he nods. A simple, broken-down bob. "Suit yourself."

He walks past me. To his truck.

COLLABORATIVE EFFORT

We take his battered Ford shortbed. It would've been more appropriate to have ridden in his Chevelle, but that would've taken a mechanical miracle.

I'm fine simply using my imagination. I've been getting the hang of it lately.

The foot-well is filled with a bedding of empty coffee cups. Candy bar wrappers. A beer can rolls between my feet.

The dashboard has a few too many parking tickets stuffed into the windshield, bleached by the sun by now. A cigarette burn bores a hole in the upholstery of my seat. I had to brush off a few fast food bags just to sit.

There's a toolbox rattling behind the driver's side seat, speckled in paint drippings. More beer cans. Tossed hamburger wrappers.

Walt hasn't said much since we started driving.

Neither have I. I'm finding myself at a loss for words. Having thought this through to a point, I never expected I'd make it this far. Where do we go from here?

I settle into my seat and think about my sensory writing exercises. Time to focus on the touch, taste, sight, sound and smell of things surrounding me.

The windshield has a single crack running the length of the glass. A crystalline lightning bolt.

Stale hamburger grease lingers in the air. It's heavy. Dense. There's cigarette smoke soaked into the upholstery. I taste it at the back of my throat. I'm having a craving for a Pal Mal like something serious. Haven't itched for a cigarette in years.

Walt must pick up on my hankering. One addict to another, I guess. He pulls out a pack from his chest pocket and silently offers me one.

How can I turn him down?

"Thanks," I say.

He doesn't reply. Merely tugs a cigarette out for himself with his lips, then tosses the pack onto the dash beside a squashed carton. He presses the lighter plug in, letting that cigarette dangle from his mouth while we both wait.

"Fucking Alan," he mutters, more to himself than for me. "Always pissing in his pants something like this might happen."

So this is it. At long last.

Story time.

I sit back and listen. "Had to lay him up pretty good just to keep his trap shut," he says. "If he went yapping about what happened, I told him he was next."

The lighter pops. Walt plucks it out and lights his own cigarette, taking a deep inhale before handing the plug to me.

"He drifted away," Walt hesitates. Smoke drifts out from his mouth. "After what happened. Knocked Leslie up a month later, so he had an excuse now. But me and Johnny knew better. That son of bitch had always been so pussy-whipped. That wasn't anything new. Now—well, now he was just plain scared."

Scared of what? I want to ask. *What would you boys have to be so afraid of?*

Of getting caught? Of what they'd done?

Of me?

"Just as well," Walt takes another drag. "I'd see him around town. Market or the bar. He could hardly look me in the eye."

The smoke settles into my lungs. The nicotine washes over me and I'm realizing it's been far too long since I've had a cigarette. Races right for my head. There's a hum in my skull now, a dizzy spell working its way over me.

The smoke adds depth to my chest. Fills the negative space within. There's a presence inside, independent of me. A ghost overtaking my bones.

Billy is here. I feel him.

I can't hold him for long. The smoke's too much for me. I try keeping my grip for as long as I can, but now I'm coughing him from my lungs.

I roll down my window and get rid of some phlegm. Get some air.

Walt's looking at me like I'm some kid taking his first puff. Like I'm some fifteen-year-old pretending to know what I'm doing and making a fool out of myself in the process. Like I can't hold my own smoke. He shakes his head, chuckling.

"Always knew Alan was gonna be the one," Walt says between inhales. "Truth told, I figured he would've clocked out a long time ago. Only a matter of time."

"Was it because of Leslie?"

He turns to me for a brief up-down. First time since we've been driving. It's a simple side-glance, eyes rolling over my way, as if to say—*The hell do you think?*

"That cow." He shakes his head. "Flirted with just about anybody who gave her the time of day. Swear to Christ, she would've shacked up with any son of bitch dumb enough to fall for her shit. She dragged Alan into all this in the first place."

"Billy fell for her."

Walt shrugs. *What can you do?* Guess he doesn't have much to say about that.

"They've got—what? Three kids? Ugly fuckers. She got what she wanted. Noosed Alan with a baby before they even graduated. She never let up. Nagging for more of this, more of that. Not for nothing, sir, but… I think your boy got off lucky."

I let this slide. *Just let him talk,* I say to myself. *Let him speak his piece.*

Billy and I want to hear his side of the story.

"We were at the dance. Been in the parking lot for about an hour. Alan had promised Leslie he'd go with her. We gave him shit for it, so he bailed. Boy, was she pissed… That bitch sure could throw a hissy-fit when she wanted to. Chewed him out right there in front of us. Fucking funny is what it was. She's just laying right into him—*You promised me, you promised me, you promised.* Put him in a mood all night."

I stare out the passenger side window as I listen. Just watch the world slide on by. Dusk is already upon us. Where did the day go? It'll be dark before long.

There's not much to see beyond a cluster of shopping centers. The names change at every intersection, but it's the same hotchpotch of options. Gas station. Hamburger joint. Supermarket. Gas station. Pizza joint. Auto repair shop.

"We'd been ragging on Alan all night," Walt says. "Really worked him up into a lather. Billy says he needed to go inside for a piss, so he steps out of the car—"

"Stop," I interrupt. "How would you know?"

"What do you mean? Billy told us. *I need to piss,* he said. Could've just gone in the parking lot, in between cars like the rest of us, but he went inside."

"...The rest?"

"Yeah. Me, Alan, and Johnny. He'd been in the car with us all night."

This doesn't feel right.

The confusion comes quick, plays across my face. I must've winced. Walt must think I don't understand, so he keeps talking. "By the time folks were filing out from the dance, Alan was ready to slap her. We'd egged it on all night. *What kinda candy-ass lets her girlfriend talk to him like that?* There was no sign of Billy. We figured that asshole—no offense—bailed on us. Wouldn't have been the first time."

First time? What is he talking about?

First time for what?

"Me and Johnny just follow Alan inside, ready to watch him have at it with Leslie. Ringside seats! They're playing the last song and—well, what've we got here? Your son's slow-dancing with Leslie. In front of everybody. He played Alan. He'd side-stepped us all so he could make a pass at his girl... They're pressing up against each other, rubbing each other. You believe that? In front of Alan. Shit, man—in front of the whole goddamn town!"

The shopping centers dissipate. The intersections stretch out further and further away from one another, until we finally hit a fresh stretch of open field.

The interstate is less developed here. Less clutter. Less lights. Now we're driving into the tree-line, surrounded by woods on either side.

Into the dark.

"Alan was ready to clock Billy right there on the dance floor. Took some nerve to pull one over on Alan like that. Like he wasn't gonna see it. His own friend."

Friend. Alan Reynolds was not Billy's *friend.*

Walt Thompson was not his *friend.*

My son was—

My son—

"Alan headed straight for him, but me and Johnny held him back. I did. *Hold up, hold up,* I say. *Not here…*"

The story comes so easily for him. Like this all happened just yesterday. There's no hiccup in his recollection, no struggle to find the memory. It's all there for him, intact, as clear and succinct as a movie he's seen a dozen times.

I envy him. This ease of his. Spinning this yarn of my boy. While I've had nothing but struggle, years of wrestling with my own memory.

He knows Billy better than I do. This story of my son is his—and I want it. *Need* it. He has no right to have kept it from me all these years. It belongs to me.

Billy belongs to *me.*

"We waited in the parking lot. Billy wandered out of the rec center by himself a little bit later. He thought we'd ditched him…"

"That's not how it happened." I blurt it out abruptly enough that Walt looks my way, take me in.

"I'm sorry," he says. "Were you there?"

How am I supposed to answer that? He's right. I wasn't. But his version bristles against mine. Rings discordantly in my mind, like hearing someone sing a familiar song, only to mix up the lyrics.

That's not how it goes…

We've arrived.

The sun sets behind the husk of this strip mall, sinking into the surrounding trees. The bare branches are veins contrasting against the dull red of the night sky.

It's dark now. Walt flips on his high beams, casting light across the parking lot. What we see before us is a wasteland. The asphalt has cracked. Weeds reach out from the fissures. The cement sinks into the ground, overwhelmed with crabgrass.

The storefronts are shuttered. The signs have been removed, exposing the electrical work, wires and busted fluorescent tubes.

Most windows have been boarded up. The few that haven't are shattered. Cracks in the glass look like cobwebs.

This used to be a Chinese food restaurant. A mildewing stack of menus are left on the floor.

This used to be a ninety-nine-cent store. A handmade sign dangles from the ceiling, swaying gently in the evening breeze, like someone hung themselves all the way out here and nobody ever found them—ALL TOOTHPASTE $1.99.

This used to be a kids' clothing shop. A mannequin

no bigger than a ten-year-old rests on its back. There's no gender to it. No hair. It's not wearing any clothes. One of their legs is missing. Both arms reach up to the ceiling, a blank look on their face, as if to appeal to the heavens. But there's nothing up there.

Walt parks over the painted lines. We're the only ones here, so it's not as if he needs to park in the appropriate spot. Still, it bothers me. The presumptuousness of it all. The parameters don't apply to him. Not here, not anywhere.

The light poles hanging over the lot haven't clicked on yet. Probably won't ever again. Why would they? Not as if there's anything out here to see.

The only light comes from Walt's truck. The high beams reach across the lot, grazing the storefronts before us.

"It was all for shits and giggles," Walt says. He puts the truck in park and sits back. He still won't look at me, talking to his windshield instead. To the strip mall.

Anything but me.

"Not like we had *a plan*. We figured we'd take him for a little spin, get him to piss in his pants, then drop him off by the side of the road. Let him hoof back home."

"Was he afraid?" I ask. "When he got into the car?"

Walt considers this. "He must've known we were up to something. Shit, he should've known. That boy fucked up. Alan loved her. You don't stab your own pal in the back by fooling around with his girl... If I were in his shoes, I woulda booked it."

Billy wasn't afraid. That's something to hold on to.

"He hopped in. Said something like—*Thought you'd left without me.* I made a crack—*We thought you'd fallen into the shitter.* I offered him the bottle and he—"

This stops me. "That's not true."

"Of course, it's true! He was taking heavy swigs along with the rest of us." Did I not know that? How could I not know that?

Now it comes back to me: The coroner's report had his blood alcohol level at 0.05%. More than enough to impair his reasoning. Enough to lower his inhibitions.

How could I forget?

A book isn't written, it's rewritten.

It's not that I had forgotten... I chose not to include it.

I'm revising history. Adjusting the facts to fit my own narrative. If a detail doesn't end up in *The Book of Billy*, then it might as well never have happened.

Selective memory. Revisionism.

Revise, revise, revise.

"Speaking of which..." Walt leans over, reaching under his seat. He fumbles for a moment before bringing back a bottle of brown liquid. It sloshes around the bottom as he unscrews the cap. He suddenly remembers his manners, "You mind...?"

I offer no response, which is enough of a

confirmation for Walt. "Happy hour somewhere," he mutters as he brings the bottle to his lips and sips.

I get lost in the phrase for a moment. The word choice.

Happy hour. What I wouldn't give for an hour—just one—of happiness.

Walt lets out the slightest belch and takes me in, like I'm something to scrutinize now. The light from the dash casts a murky green glow across his face. He looks sick to me. His body has loosened up over these last few years. His muscles have lost their grip.

He holds out the bottle. There's barely any left. We could finish it between us in a few sips. Everything within me begs for that bottle. I can feel the gravitational pull toward it. My eyes settle in on the last inch of amber liquid and I can't help but think of myself suspended in it for centuries, some prehistoric mosquito.

"No."

"Suit yourself." He shrugs and polishes it off. He holds it up to the dim light just to make sure there's nothing left. "Billy made sure to bogart the bottle. Shrewd move on his part. He was no dumbass, even if he was a dumb-shit. Starts flipping the bottle over in his hand. Grips the neck, flips it in the air, catches it. Does it two or three times. He flips it one more time, catches that Johnny Walker by the neck and then he smashes me flat in the face with it—while I'm fucking driving."

"That's a lie."

"Says who? *You*? His *daddy*?"

"He'd never do something like that. You're lying—"

"Don't take this the wrong way, sir, but I seriously suggest you ask yourself just who in the hell you think your son was. Sure as shit wasn't some Boy Scout."

"You didn't know him."

"You didn't, either! That puts us in the same boat, now—don't it?"

"You're lying," I say. "You're making this up."

"You're one to talk." He huffs. "I ain't the one making up stories about my boy and reading them to everybody. You're the one out here spreading lies—"

"Fuck you."

"Don't start acting all high and mighty on me, man! Your son was no better than us. He was just like us, you hear? He was our friend. At least we thought so…"

"Stop lying!"

"I'm telling it to you straight! Got no reason to lie, now, do I? What've I got left? There's no skin in the game. It would be water under the bridge by now… but the water's all dried up!"

I'm silent, so he continues.

"You never noticed my nose, did you? Your fucking son broke it. I was black and blue for a week. He smashed me in the face so good, I nearly lost control of the wheel. Blacked out for a second. He grabs the wheel and yanks on it, like the bastard wanted to run us all right off the road."

"That's not true," I say with what strength I have left.

"Why would I lie? What'd be the point? You got me, I'm here, so *let's do this*. Let's air it all out. But I'm not sugar-coating this shit for you. You want it, you got it. But you're gonna hear it exactly the way it happened. That clear?"

I nod.

"Your son would've killed all of us. Crazy cocksucker. He would've done it, too, if it weren't for Alan grabbing hold of his seatbelt and yanking him back."

No.

"Your boy wouldn't let up. Kept at it. Punching the fuck out me. My face. My chest. He was some fucking rabid dog let loose in my car."

No, please. Not Billy. Not like this.

Not my boy.

Not you…

"We've got to wrestle him. Hold him back. And still—*still*—that son of a bitch kept at us. Kicking the windshield. Biting at Alan's hand. Never seen anything like it."

This is not how the story is supposed to end.

This is not the story in my head.

I take in the parking lot. See the weeds reaching out from the cracked asphalt. See them gripping the tires of the car and pulling us under. See them weave around my body, gripping my bones and refusing to let go. Pulling me down into the dirt.

It takes me a moment to realize Walt is staring at me. Taking me in. "Why are you doing this to yourself?"

"It's all I have," I say. *What else is there? What else have you left me?*

Walt grunts. That's all it takes. He gets it on some primal level. A man needs to know. Needs to see it through. To the very end. No matter where it takes him, no matter how far down to hell it drags him. No matter how much it hurts. No matter what it does to his body, his soul—he must see it through.

The truth is there for those foolish enough to find it.

The truth will set you free.

To hell with that. The truth empties you out. Leaves you hollow.

A shell.

"The tape was in the back seat." It must feel good for Walt. *Liberating,* even. Getting this off his chest. After all these years. "Alan grabbed it. It was his idea. Wasn't like we discussed it amongst ourselves beforehand. He reached for it and—"

He hesitates. I'm not breathing, hanging off every word. I can't move.

"And the rest of us just follow along."

He looks to me, absolved, as if that's the end of the

story. That's as far as he's willing to go. He probably thinks this is enough for me. That I've had my fill.

"Show me." It comes out loud. Sturdy. There's no plea to it. I surprise even myself by saying it as forcefully as I do, but I'm not giving him an option.

Walt looks at me like he doesn't understand.

I nod to the backseat.

Walt follows. He turns and finds the toolbox behind him. Hesitates.

"Christ," he mutters, "you're one fucked up old man. You know that?"

"Show me. I want to see."

What he must be thinking is anybody's guess. What could possibly be going through his mind?

I can't rightfully say for certain I know what I'm even thinking. The two of us have gone beyond explanation. There's no rationalization for what we're doing.

This is our story. We're collaborating now.

Co-authors.

Walt reaches back and opens the toolbox. He pushes past the monkey wrench and loose drill bits. He pulls back the top compartment to expose a lower cavity full of tools. A hammer. Box cutter.

And a half-used roll of duct tape. Silver tinsel-strength. I know the brand. Sturdy stuff. Good for all kinds of weather.

Walt grabs the roll with his index finger, hooking it. When he brings it up front, he starts to absentmindedly spin it with his finger, twirling like a hula-hoop.

"This is what you're after?" He asks. I can hear the dare in there, slithering through the words like a snake in the grass. "This is what you really want?"

I nod. *Yes. God, yes...* This is what I want.

The tape hasn't stopped spinning around his finger. It twirls faster.

Faster.

Faster.

I get dizzy. I'm hypnotized. I could fly off right then and there.

Walt finally nods, takes a breath. He grips the tape, quickly, like a snake locking its jaws around an unsuspecting mouse, his hands grasping at the roll to stop its spin—and in that moment, the world stops turning.

Everything just halts.

Walt peels off a six-inch stretch of duct tape. The familiar rip tears away from the rest of the roll.

It sounds so welcoming.

Inviting.

Walt holds the tape up to me. Presents the adhesive side to me.

Final warning, his eyes seem to say. He waits, letting this sink in. Probably more for my sake than his, but still, I can see his wrist tremble by just a fraction.

"Show me," I say.

I stare down the gray expanse, the vast fog in his hands.

"Here goes nothing." Walt brings the tape over my eyes, sealing me in.

The darkness is infinite. The world, my life up to this point, the last forty years of borrowed time, are eclipsed.

I'm not alone. Something shifts in the black.

What took you so long, Dad?

EXQUISITE CORPSE

I hear Walt's door slam shut from within the darkness. I'm left fidgeting in the gray, this fog of duct tape swallowing everything. I don't know where he is anymore. He's slipped away from my senses. I can't hear him. Can't see. Can't—

A rush of cold air spills over me as my door swings open.

"Get out," Walt says inches away from my ear. I'm not moving fast enough for him. Before I can resist, his fingers wrap around my arm, gripping the bicep tightly—and I find myself lifting off, flung out from the truck, launched into the air.

I must feel so light to him. My body is nothing but a bundle of kindling, a slender assortment of bones barely tethered together by this wrinkled wrapping of skin.

My foot finds the asphalt, but it won't hold the rest

of me up. I can't stand on my own yet. I'm wobbling. Toppling over.

"Watch it," Walt says. I end up collapsing into him. My shoulder strikes his chest. I think it's his chest. I rebound right off him.

I can feel myself falling. The air whisks on by as I spin through the air.

"Christ." Walt grabs my arm and my body halts. I'm suspended in mid-air, dangling over some massive precipice. If Walt lets go, I'd end up falling forever.

"Easy now." Walt brings me upright. Both feet find the sturdy ground. I'm a mannequin to him. A wooden doll to position however he'd like. I think of the child's dummy in the clothing store, how we'd make a great pair. If Walt were to leave me next to it, posing us together, we could stay out here for the rest of our lives. Two shop dummies, father and son, left to the weather and elements.

"Come on."

In the gray, I find myself fighting off this feeling that the parking lot has become much vaster than it actually is. I could be in the desert right now. The tundra. Miles of open terrain. The landscape has expanded beyond my blindfold and yet every step feels as if I'm at the edge of a cliff. One wrong move and I'll plummet.

"Come on."

His voice is much more guttural in the gray, buried under phlegm and fat. The words are laced in alcohol. I can smell every command better than I can hear them.

"Come on."

Walt forces me forward. Smacks my shoulder and sends me stumbling deeper into the gray. My steps are tentative, but he won't let me slow down. Dragging me across the lot.

"Here."

I'm ashamed at how light I am. How weak.

"Stop."

There's no resistance in me. I have no fight.

"On your knees." Walt tugs my arm down. I've got no choice but to drop.

My knees make impact with the cement. The pain is so sudden, a jolt through my bones, I can't help but cry out.

"You asked for it, old man. Remember that."

I did. I asked for this.

I am here. Lost in the vast expanse of gray. But where's Billy? He was just with me a moment ago. In the truck. My eyes are pressed shut by the duct tape. I can feel the adhesive clinging to my eyelids. If I try to open them, the flesh tugs back.

I can't open my eyes. There are so many shadows here in the gray. I must be facing the truck. I think I feel the warmth of headlights spreading across my cheeks.

Or maybe I'm just imagining it. My senses struggle to adjust to my newfound handicap, overcompensating for the abrupt blindness.

"I told Alan to make sure his nose was free to breathe," Walt announces from somewhere off to my left. I think it's my left. Maybe he's behind me now? "He said there was an airway. Billy was breathing, as far as we all could tell."

The words are coming from some elevated space over my head. Walt must be standing above me now. Beside me? Behind? I can't hear as well as I hoped. Then again, everything for Billy at this point would've been muted under that mask of duct tape. Nothing would've reached his ears by now.

"Billy kept grabbing at his head," Walt says. "Kept trying to pull the tape away, so I had to bat at his hands. Smack them back. When that didn't work, I popped a squat on him. Pinning him in place for a bit, just to fuck with him."

There's a weight pressing against my chest. A grain sack. A cement bag.

A boy.

A seventeen-year-old Walt Thompson is squatting on top of me. I try to push him off, but he keeps batting my hands away. I don't know where to grab, where to gain some grip and force him off. He's everywhere and nowhere all at once.

I can't push him away.

Can't get him off.

Can't get up.

"He'd brought this upon himself, Mr. Partridge. You understand that, right? We were just messing with him… but things just got outta hand."

The weight of him.

He's crushing me.

I can feel my ribcage piercing my lungs. The air can't reach them anymore.

"All we wanted was for him to cry uncle, you know? I'd give it another second. Just another second for him to squirm and then I'd get up…"

I'm going to suffocate in here.

I'm going to die.

"We didn't mean for any of this to happen. Hand to God. He just—he just stopped moving. Just stopped. I jumped up and gave him a nudge and…"

The gray is deepening, darkening. The shadows swell, saturating the tape. It washes over.

"I'm sorry, Mr. Partridge. Honestly. We didn't know…"

The words are fading.

"…didn't know he would…"

Fainter now.

"…so we just left…"

Walt is still talking, but the words are muffled now. There's nothing to hear except for the fresh strip of duct tape peeling off the roll. Slowly, at first. Tauntingly. The unwrapping gains momentum, tearing away faster. Faster. That persistent rip weaves around my head. It covers my mouth. My left cheek, then the right. My ears. My hair. The back of my head. I can feel the roll orbit my skull, rotating around my head. It presses against my cheeks, cinching against my skin, like a snake coiling around my head and constricting as it sheds layer after layer after layer of tape.

Burying me.

—

Not tape.

An engine. Walt must've climbed back in his truck, turning the ignition over.

By the time I tug the tape away from my eyes, he's gone. The truck taillights drift down the interstate, slipping off into the tree line and disappearing for good.

I'm alone in the parking lot.

The brittle asphalt crumbles underneath me. I strain to sit up, feel the pain in my spine. The sting is still in my knees.

The roll of duct tape rests next to me. He barely used it. Six inches over my eyes.

I imagined the rest.

It's dark now. No headlights to illuminate the lot. No engine idling. It's peaceful. I can hear the swell of crickets chirruping from the surrounding woods.

The police didn't come upon Billy's body until the morning, still several hours from now—so I decide to sit here and wait for the sunrise. Sit in this stillness.

In the quiet.

UNRELIABLE NARRATOR

"Anything new in the Partridge case?"

I don't even know if there's anyone listening on the other end of the line nowadays, but I ask the question anyhow.

Why dial the police station anymore when I can simply call upon my muse?

Anything new?

Anything?

Did I know my son? Did I make him up? If I did, what does that make me?

Carol and I inhabit different corners of the house now. There are days when we don't see each other. Days can slip by without us speaking to one another.

Words are precious things. I don't have many left. All mine go into the book.

Everybody's got at least one good book in them.

My book's about Billy.

There are chapters of his life that I have to add. Memories that pop up out of the blue. I've got to catch them. Scribble them down before they can disappear again.

There's a chance new information will come to light, some tiny detail.

There's always more story to tell. So much to edit. Revise until it finally makes sense. And if a fact doesn't fit, can you fault me for fixing it? Rewriting the past?

My hands aren't as nimble as they used to be. My penmanship is unraveling, the letters loosening. But I've got to keep writing.

The photo album's burgundy cover ripped. The binding has worn down so much, it finally tore free. Have to reinforce it with some duct tape, just to keep it together.

With that roll in my hand, I end up peeling off an extra strip for myself. I tug a couple inches, then a couple more, winding the roll around my forearm.

Then up to my elbow. My bicep.

I keep going. My chest. Waist. I don't want to stop. *Can't.* I started something and I need to see it through, reaching—

the end

—of the roll before finding a fresh one.

One last strip for my eyes. The living room disappears. It's so dark in here.

Welcome back, Dad, Billy whispers right in my ear.

A work of art is never finished, our sage instructor once said. *Only abandoned.*

I'm not about to abandon my boy.

ACKNOWLEDGMENTS

This story was partially inspired by "Persistence of a Father Brings News in a Killing," written by Erica Goode, The New York Times, May 8, 2011.

Thanks to Kevin Confoy, Edward Allan Baker and my fellow writing instructors who shepherded the stories of so many writers at the Sarah Lawrence College Summer Writing Intensive throughout the years. Those stories live on.

Thanks to Doug Murano for bringing this story to Bad Hand Books. Eternal gratitude goes to you for everything you've done.

Thanks to Eddie Gamarra for asking for a new Liam Neeson vehicle all those years ago… and getting this instead.

Thanks to Nick McCabe and everyone at The Gotham Group.

Thanks to Michael Hartman and everyone at Ziffren Brittenham LLP.

Thanks to my family. To Indrani, Jasper and Cormac.

Thanks to you for reading, always reading.

ABOUT THE AUTHOR

CLAY MCLEOD CHAPMAN writes books, comic books, children's books, as well as for film and television. His most recent novels include *What Kind of Mother* and *Ghost Eaters*. You can find him at www.claymcleodchapman.com.

CLAY McLEOD CHAPMAN

Printed in the United States
by Baker & Taylor Publisher Services